"I found myself dreaming Carter, of Dejah Thoris, of T. Woola...

"But the rest is in the manuscript that... I have found the means to transmit to you with this letter. You and a few others of the chosen will believe in it—for the rest it matters not as yet. The time will come..."

—Excerpted from a letter to Edgar Rice Burroughs from Ulysses Paxton, dated Helium, June 8, 1925, in *The Master Mind of Mars*

A GUIDE TO BARSOOM

Eleven Sections of References in One Volume Dealing with the
Martian Stories Written by Edgar Rice Burroughs

Compiled by
JOHN FLINT ROY

ReAnimus Press

Breathing Life into Great Books

ReAnimus Press
1100 Johnson Road #16-143
Golden, CO 80402
www.ReAnimus.com

http://ReAnimus.com/authors/johnflintroy

Cover Art by Neal MacDonald

ISBN-13: 978-0615687315

10 9 8 7 6 5 4 3 2 1

Publisher's Note

John Flint Roy did a tremendous job in cataloging all the aspects of Barsoom, and we at ReAnimus Press were sorry to see that it was out of print for so long—and we're now excited that we can bring it back to life! Some notes on our reanimation are in order.

We have endeavored to reproduce JFR's compendium without errors. Although we feel it is as error-free as we can make it, it is unlikely we have met that goal 100%. If you detect any typographical errors, please relay them to us via our web site, www.ReAnimus.com, so that we may fix them in updated editions. To sweeten the pot, we'll offer a 10% off coupon per new error, good for any one of our other titles in our store. We'll also maintain an errata sheet on the site at www.ReAnimus.com/barsoom for errors we've been made aware of (and have either fixed in later versions or will be fixed in the next).

We also want to thank Jim Sullos of ERB, Inc., the Disney corporation, Camille "Caz" Cazedessus, and Neal MacDonald for making this book possible.

Thanks, and enjoy the book!

—Dr. Andrew Burt
Publisher
ReAnimus Press

Contents

List of Illustrations

In order of appearance:

Introduction to the 2012 Edition

I came into science fiction fandom through the Burroughs door about half a century ago, and John F. Roy was my guide and my dear friend for many years. (Not many people know, or remember, that he was a Royal Canadian Mountie when he wasn't being the preeminent Edgar Rice Burroughs scholar of our time. He looked really heroic in his red jacket and Dudley Do-Right hat, sitting atop his horse.)

Burroughs created Barsoom with "Under the Moons of Mars", literally a century ago, but it took another 64 years before the field produced someone competent enough to create the book you are now reading. And given the popularity of Barsoom, it *needed* to be created. Burroughs created a reasonably consistent world over the span of 10+ novels, including a language (or at least a number of words that were used with some degree of consistency), a history, a background, customs, weapons, scientific innovations and scientific shortcomings, and a few resident races. It took someone with John's thoroughness and dedication to codify it all, as he does in the pages up ahead.

And another need for this book is that there are some areas in which Burroughs wasn't *that* consistent. Ask anyone who's ever tried to create a map of Barsoom about that (and believe me, back in the 1960s, a *lot* of us took a crack at it, with no two maps coming out the same.)

John shared his expertise with Burroughs fans through a seemingly endless series of scholarly articles in the leading Burroughs fanzines of the time, primarily Camille Cazedessus's *ERB-dom*, which to this day remains the only Burroughs zine ever to win a Hugo. He had no interest in writing sequels, as so many others did. He was a scholar, and all of his considerable talent was channeled into that pursuit.

How high was the field's regard for his expertise? Back in 1964 I wrote a 28,000-word sequel to *Llana of Gathol* (with ERB, Inc.'s authorization, of course). There was a stipulation: it couldn't be printed until John vetted it for stylistic and factual consistency, and gave it his approval, which he did after I made the changes he stipulated.

I have many wonderful memories of John and his lovely and loving wife Ev. Ev wasn't much interested in Burroughs, science fiction, or conventions, but she encouraged John to pursue his interest, always accompanied him, and usually spent her days touring and sightseeing in whatever city the convention happened to be, then joining him for dinner and the evening parties. I remember one Worldcon, the 1966 Tricon, where I stayed up so late each night that I slept right through the alarm every morning, and I expressed the fear that I'd do it again on getaway day, and that Carol (who had been unable to wake me and get me moving in much less than half an hour) and I would miss our train home. So at 6:00 AM the phone rings, I groggily pick it up, and John begins reciting the silliest damned Burroughesque nonsense rhyme I'd ever heard...and in a couple of minutes I was laughing so hard that I stayed awake the rest of the morning and we caught our train.

He was a good and decent man. The Burroughs field doubtless misses its finest scholar, but nowhere near as much as I miss my wonderful Canadian friend. I cherish my first edition of this book, with John's inscription and the wonderful Neal MacDonald illustrations, but not as much as I cherish my memories of John himself.

— Mike Resnick

Introduction

When Edgar Rice Burroughs (1875-1950) wrote "Dejah Thoris, A Princess of Mars," in 1911, he had no idea that he was opening a new era in the science fiction field. His account of fifteen-foot green men, eight-legged beasts, oviparous females, and sword-swinging red men was an immediate success, and the public clamored for more.

Over a period of thirty years (1911–1941), Burroughs wrote ten Martian tales and started on the eleventh. It is obvious to the discerning reader that he did not have a long-range plan for this series, but rather wrote each story as it came to him; and then had to fit each into the pattern set by the earlier tales. This did not always work, thus leading to various and sometimes regrettable inconsistencies. Had he realized how popular this series would become and that he would be called upon for more and more tales from Barsoom, he no doubt would have drawn up a firmer set of rules and stuck to them.

Consistent or conflicting, the story of life and death, romance and tragedy, on the Red Planet is undoubtedly one of the greatest science-fiction series of all time. Taking the planet Mars as a basis, Burroughs created a world of dead seabeds, towering mountains, polar ice caps, underground rivers, weird plants, beautiful flowers, and strange beasts. He peopled it with four different human races and one semi-human. He gave it a history, several phases of civilization, and an assortment of religions. He added dauntless heros, beautiful maidens, evil villains, and fearful monsters—all the ingredients necessary for a series of thrilling adventures on any world.

Following is a list of the eleven Burroughs Mars, or Barsoom, works—when and how they appeared first, and were named:

1. *A Princess of Mars*
   First book publication: 1917 – A.C. McClurg
   First magazine appearance: "Under the Moons of Mars" – Feb.-July, 1912 – *The All-Story*

2. *The Gods of Mars*

> First book publication: 1918 – A.C. McClurg
>
> First magazine appearance: "The Gods of Mars" – Jan.-May, 1913 – *The All-Story*

3. *The Warlord of Mars*

> First book publication: 1919 – A.C. McClurg
>
> First magazine appearance: "Warlord of Mars" – Dec., 1913 to Mar., 1914 – *The All-Story*

4. *Thuvia, Maid of Mars*

> First book publication: 1920 – A.C. McClurg
>
> First magazine appearance: "Thuvia, Maid of Mars" – Apr. 8-22, 1916 – *All-Story Weekly*

5. *The Chessmen of Mars*

> First book publication: 1922 – A.C. McClurg
>
> First magazine appearance: "Chessmen of Mars" – Feb. 18 to Apr. 1, 1922 – *Argosy All-Story Weekly*

6. *The Master Mind of Mars*

> First book publication: 1928 – A.C. McClurg
>
> First magazine appearance: "The Master Mind of Mars" – July 15, 1927 – *Amazing Stories Annual*

7. *A Fighting Man of Mars*

> First book publication: 1931 – Metropolitan
>
> First magazine appearance: "A Fighting Man of Mars" – Apr.-Sep., 1930 – *Blue Book* magazine

8. *Swords of Mars*

> First book publication: 1936 – Burroughs
>
> First magazine appearance: "Swords of Mars" – Nov., 1934 to Apr. 1935 – *Blue Book* magazine

9. *Synthetic Men of Mars*

      First book publication: 1940 – Burroughs

      First magazine appearance: "The Synthetic Men of Mars"
– Jan. 7 to Feb. 11, 1939 – *Argosy*

10. *Llana of Gathol*

      First book publication: 1948 – Burroughs

      First magazine appearance:

        "The City of Mummies" – Mar., 1941 – *Amazing Stories*
        "Black Pirates of Barsoom" – Jun., 1941 – *Amazing Stories*
        "Yellow Men of Mars" – Aug., 1941 – *Amazing Stories*
        "Invisible Men of Mars" – Oct., 1941 – *Amazing Stories*

10. *John Carter of Mars*

      First book publication: 1964 – Canaveral

      First magazine appearance:

        "John Carter and the Giant of Mars" – Jan., 1941 – *Amazing Stories*

        "Skeleton Men of Jupiter" – Feb., 1943 – *Amazing Stories*

That Burroughs read and made use of Percival Lowell's books *Mars and Its Canals* and *Mars as the Abode of Life* cannot be denied; and definitely he perused newspaper articles and Sunday supplements dealing with the Red Planet. Thus it was that he wrote of a Mars patterned on the facts and theories of the day. To these he added his own embellishments, caring little, at that time, about their credibility. In later books, he felt obliged to change certain of his details because some theories had been readjusted by the scientific world. Many of Burroughs' improvisations, however, remained untouched because they were necessary to his story. They were what distinguished John Carter's Barsoom from Lowell's Mars.

Listed hereunder are the eleven titles of the Mars series, together with the abbreviations which will be used for them throughout this *Guide*. Reference will be by chapter number only, rather than page, in view of the differences among the various editions now available. For example, *PM/3* means *A Princess of Mars,* Chapter 3.

1. *A Princess of Mars*   *(PM)*
2. *The Gods of Mars*   *(GM)*
3. *The Warlord of Mars*   *(WM)*
4. *Thuvia, Maid of Mars*   *(TMM)*
5. *The Chessmen of Mars*   *(CM)*
6. *The Master Mind of Mars*   *(MMM)*
7. *A Fighting Man of Mars*   *(FMM)*
8. *Swords of Mars*   *(SM)*
9. *Synthetic Men of Mars*   *(SMM)*
10. *Llana of Gathol*   *(LG)*
11. *John Carter of Mars*   *(JCM(SMJ))*

Insofar as the last title is concerned, I will deal only with the second part, "Skeleton Men of Jupiter," as I feel that "John Carter and the Giant of Mars" is not one of the canon but is merely an imaginative bit of fiction featuring John Carter, and of questionable authorship.

The first part of the *Guide* is a brief history of Barsoom from its beginning up to the time of Carter's arrival on that world. It should explain some of the points not adequately covered by Burroughs when editing the voluminous notes given him by his uncle one August day in 1898, in a hotel room in Richmond, Virginia.

Chapter I – A Brief History of Pre-Carter Barsoom

It floated there in space, fourth from the giant sun, slowly turning on its axis. Its rolling hills and blue waters were silent and empty. On that entire world only one spot pulsed with the mysterious spark of life. It was in the Valley Dor, and the stirring was within the great Tree of Life.

All this was some twenty-three million years ago, when Dor lay astride the planet's equator.

The millennia passed.

The sun was much smaller and cooler now, and over the eons the axis of the planet had shifted. The once-tropical Valley Dor now lay at the south pole and the Tree of Life was dead, its work accomplished. From it had come the hideous plant man, the sixteen-legged worm, the ancestor of the white ape, and the first man.

The black races of Barsoom say the first man was dark-skinned and that he released the other types of creatures from whom "sprang every other form of animal life upon Barsoom." Soon the oceans swarmed with fish, the air sang to the sound of birds and insects, while the land sheltered and nourished all forms of creatures, furred and scaled, multi-limbed and biped, savage and gentle. As was pre-destined, the biped became the dominant species, and in time it ruled the land.

Three races of man came into being: the darkskinned ones, who proudly claimed they were the First Born; the white-skinned, with blond or auburn hair, who looked upon the claim with skepticism; and the yellow-skinned, who said little about it.

Century after century passed into oblivion; ice ages came and went; civilizations, each greater than the last, grew and then faded away. Finally it seemed the ultimate had been attained. The Orovars, or white race, ruled most of the land and there was peace. Illness had been conquered; the life span was a thousand years. Great fleets sailed the five oceans, exchanging goods between the continents and throughout the countless islands.

Horz, capital city of Barsoom's greatest empire, was the seat of learning and culture of the most glorious race of beings a world has ever known. It was one of the busiest ports on the shores of the mighty Throxeus, rivaled only by Lothar, which lay upon the opposite shore of the same great ocean.

Kar Komak, known as "The Bowman," lived in those days. He commanded the ships of Lothar, whose sailors were unsurpassed throughout Barsoom; and he looked with scorn upon the city dwellers—such as Tario, Jeddak of Lothar—who frowned upon exertion and violence, believing that the mind was everything. Komak knew the great ships from the yards of Kam Han Tor, brother of the Jeddak of Horz, and swore no man could build them better. He knew, also, the treacherous currents outside the harbor at Aaanthor, close by the foothills of Torquas; and had visited the free port of Korad, halfway around the world from Throxeus. Equally as well did he know the quays of Xanator and Warhoon and fogbound Thark. Where a ship could sail, Kar Komak had been.

All this was more than half a million years ago.

And then it happened. The oceans began to dry up, rain ceased to fall, lakes and rivers vanished. In desperation, the great ports extended their wharves time and time again, but in vain. All shipping eventually ceased. The half-dried seas, surrounded by muddy plains, no longer held back the land-roving green hordes of four-armed giants and they stormed across a dying world.

The haughty First Born retreated along the banks of a great river, finally reaching the south polar regions, where they settled around an underground sea which they called Omean. Here they remained—and were forgotten by the outside world.

The yellow race, the bearded Okarians, turned northward, found a way through the mighty ice barrier that encircles the northern polar wastes, and were not seen again.

Among the white race, especially, there were pockets of resistance. The Lotharians, under their jeddak, Tario, fought and fled halfway across a world until they founded a new Lothar in a hidden valley deep in the Torquas Mountains. Another group—some say from Korad—headed for the south-polar ice fields and eventually carved out a home from the bowels of the Otz Mountains which surround the Sea of Koras.

A tribe of wandering blacks were turned away from the mountains of Gathol, and later from the swamplands of Toonol. Finally they made their way to the bottom of a rift deep in the floor of the now-vanished Throxeus, and here they founded Kamtol.

Countless other groups fell before the exultant green men, but the survivors regrouped time and again regardless of nation or color. In time they blended into one sturdy self-sufficient race of red-skinned warriors, and slowly but steadily won back the land from the merciless green savages.

A band of Orovars from Horz, high-ranking members of the jeddak's retinue, had refused to intermate with their newfound allies, including even whites from other cities. Eventually, when mankind was well on the ascendancy again, they quietly left their red-skinned associates and returned to the now long-deserted city. Here they rebuilt their own community secretly and in a manner that led all others to believe the once-great metropolis was still nothing more than an empty shell.

Early in the desperate years—when, on the one hand, the seas and rivers were evaporating and the atmosphere was becoming too thin to support life, and, on the other hand, the wild green hordes were sweeping over the face of the planet—it was realized that man must call upon all his ingenuity and resourcefulness if the planet were to survive. He was, as Tars Tarkas would say, "caught between the wild thoat of certainty and the mad Zitidar of fact."

One group of scientists was given the task of creating machinery which would produce atmosphere; and they did.

Another major and immediate problem was the care and transport-
ing of children and pregnant women in a world where it was necessary to be on the move constantly, either in search of food or fleeing
from the green barbarians. Scientists in the medical field had long
given thought to having their women oviparous — as were the green
women — rather than womb-bearing. What had hitherto been strictly a
moral problem became a necessity. The change was made slowly but
surely, and now the women of all branches of the human race on Barsoom are egg-laying creatures. Only minor physical changes took
place in the female form. For example, breasts were no longer needed
for nursing; however, they did remain — smaller, it is true — but still an
obvious feminine attribute. The young Martian now steps from his
shell fully developed, except in size. His education starts immediately, and within five years he is virtually mature.

The centuries continued to roll by and the struggle went on, particularly the battle against nature itself. In time, atmosphere plants
went into operation at a sufficient capacity and scientists turned their
attention to discovering sources of water and distributing that water
to all parts of the globe. The first step was simple: the melting and collecting of water from the ice caps at the two poles. Then began the
building of a series of canals across the face of Barsoom. The task
seemed almost insurmountable, but it was accomplished. It took decade after weary decade, in which there were problems of priority, of
manpower, and of material. The green men had to be convinced it
was for their good as well as that of the red men, and they had to be
persuaded not to destroy those hard-won life lines. Slowly but surely,
the red race was bringing their world back to where it was before the
debacle.

Though fortified cities were appearing across the land and nations
were withdrawing within self-defined borders, agriculture was making a comeback and trade and commerce springing up between
friendly states — war between others. Nature had not changed.

Let us now take a look at Barsoom as it was when John Carter
slipped across the void from Earth, faced a world single-handed, won
himself a mate, and became Warlord of Mars.

Chapter II – A Geography of Barsoom, Including a Gazetteer-Index and Hemispheric and Polar Maps of Its Surface

The planet Mars orbits the sun at distances ranging from 126 million miles to 152 million miles and takes almost 687 Earth days to make the trip. Its distance from our world varies from 35 million miles to 244 million. The circumference of Mars at its equator is estimated at something over 13,000 miles, and it rotates on its axis in slightly over 24 hours, Earth time. Its seasons are twice as long as Earth's. An interesting feature is that when Mars is at perihelion it always has its south pole tipped toward the sun, thus causing 160 days of summer in that region.

Mars has two satellites. Deimos is slightly over 12,000 miles distant and circles the planet once every 30 1/2 hours. Phobos is about 3700 miles out and circles Mars every 7 1/2 hours. Both moons are extremely small, Phobos being only eight or ten miles in diameter, and Deimos five or six. Because of their low altitude neither is visible from the surface of the planet at the polar regions.

For a more "intimate" report on the Red Planet, one must refer to the information supplied by that undying Virginian, John Carter, who, since 1866, spent most of his life, except for brief periods, on that distant world.

Carter's description of the planet differs in some respects from that given by scientists and scholars of Earth. Thus, we feel compelled to assume that Barsoom and Mars are not one and the same; rather, that the former occupies the same place as the latter but in another dimension. How, otherwise, could Carter have a physical body on two planets in the same solar system at the same time? Also, we can look up and see *Mars* but we cannot see *Barsoom*, whereas the people of that world can look down on us from their dimension. See *PM/11* and *MMM/9* in this regard.

One of the main points of difference will be found in the moons of Barsoom. Cluros and Thuria are the same size as Deimos and Phobos, respectively, and the same distance from the surface of their planet; however, they do not appear to follow the same east-west orbit. Instead, they seem to move in a north-south direction, for both are visible over the Thern forts in the Otz Mountains (*GM/6*) and Thuria, at least, casts her light upon the sunken Valley Dor (*WM/1*).

Let us now look at the world of Barsoom as portrayed by John Carter, Virginian, Warlord of Barsoom.

When Carter opens his eyes that morning in March, 1866 (Earth calendar), he sees before him mile upon mile of yellowish, moss-like vegetation. It spreads across a deep, circular basin until it merges into a series of low hills. Outcroppings of quartz-bearing rock show through in places. There is no sign of water nor of any growth other than moss. Beyond the hills are more hills, some reaching high enough to be considered mountains, although few peaks exceed four thousand feet.

The endless acres of yellow moss were once the beds of Barsoom's five mighty oceans and numerous seas, waters that vanished half a million years before. Rising from what were once shores are foothills, tablelands, and mountains — former continents and islands of the ancient world. No charts or maps remain among the few records available to modern man, and only the quays of the long-deserted seaports indicate where water once lapped the shore. We have an entire world of dry land, the only exceptions being some swamp or marshy areas, a few small streams, one or two rivers, and a sea at the south pole.

With the exception of the polar regions, it would appear that the ochre moss-like growth has spread across Barsoom, moving from the dry sea basins to the fertile lowlands and onto the plains, the plateaus, and even the hills themselves. Only in the very arid regions do we find naked rock and barren gullies. There are also patches of land where forests thrive, but these are few, and are highly prized by the nation within whose boundaries they exist.

The Hemispheres

Let us take a look at Barsoom from a vantage spot on Thuria, the nearer moon. Just coming into our view of Exum, which is the equivalent of Earth's Greenwich...

Exum lies on an equatorial tableland that was once covered by the waters of Throxeus, Barsoom's greatest ocean. Some 950 haads to the west can be seen the towering mountain peak of Gathol, site of one of the very few cities of ancient Barsoom still inhabited. Formerly an island in the Throxeus, Gathol is now surrounded by a great salt marsh, to the west of which lies a country of torn rocks and yawning chasms.

Due east of Exum some 5000 haads is the Forest of Lost Men, in a sunken tropical valley. Here are the two well-camouflaged and self-supporting cities, Invak and Onvak.

Some 2500 haads northeast of Exum is the city of Dusar, capital of a nation that stretches virtually from pole to pole.

Due north of Exum, almost 4000 haads, is the supposedly deserted city of Horz, the ancient Greenwich of Barsoom and capital of what was then its greatest nation.

Southwest of Horz and almost due north of Gathol, in what was once ocean, will be found a "fault," a jagged crack in the seabed. The bottom of this tremendous canyon contains at least one lake, some small streams, and the city of Kamtol, the home of a branch of the black-skinned First Born.

Some thousand or more haads to the west of Kamtol lies the city of Toonol, on the eastern edge of the Great Toonolian Marshes, which stretch some 5000 haads to the west. At the opposite end of this remnant of a seabed is the city-state of Phundahl. Morbus, where Ras Thavas rebuilt his laboratories, is in the north-central part of the marshes.

Well to the northwest of Phundahl lie the Artolian Hills, a sprawling range of snow-clad mountains, and beyond them, almost at Long. 180°, the city-state of Duhor.

Across the dead seabed, southwest from Phundahl, lies Ptarth, one of the more powerful nations of Barsoom.

Of the area above the 30th parallel North, and stretching west from Duhor to Horz—which is halfway around the globe—nothing is recorded in the Carter documents. It may be shared by Dusar, Duhor, and Ptarth or be made up of several smaller city-states. We do not know.

Somewhere far to the northwest of Horz lies the city of Raxar, of which virtually nothing is known. Further to the west, and due north of Morbus, is the city of Amhor, famous for its zoo.

Due west of Gathol, and beyond the tortuous canyons which form its western boundary, lie three small and ancient cities, Manator, Manatos, and Manataj. Well off the beaten track, isolated and independent, this tri-city state still clings to the customs of yesteryear.

Across more rough and rocky land many haads to the southwest, in an area of low hills known as Bantoom, is the home of the kaldanes, a strange offshoot of mankind, a brain with a head but no body. For transportation it has developed the rikor, a humanoid body, headless and almost incapable of independent action.

Far to the southeast, around the 50th parallel South, will be found
the city of Tjanath, and a deep and narrow gorge called the Valley
Hohr, wherein lies the castle of Ghasta. A few hundred haads northeast of Tjanath is the ancient castle of Jhama. Somewhere between this
group and Bantoom is the little-known city of Kobol. Well to the east
of Jhama, and a bit north, is Jahar, not far from the Mountains of Torquas. U-Gor, a southern province of Jahar, was once rich farmland but
is now a desert.

Deep in a hidden valley within the Torquas range is the city of Lothar, the inhabitants of which are direct descendants of ancient Lothar, the great seaport that flourished a million years before on the
shores of the Throxeus Ocean, half a world to the north.

Xanator and Aaanthor, two deserted cities of ancient Barsoom, lie
north and south respectively of the Torquas Mountains. The area to
the east and north is the home of savage green men, the Torquasians,
whose headquarters are in the once-great city of Torquas; to their
south roam their bitter enemies, the Thurds, another green tribe.

Due east of Torquas some 2000 haads lie the twin cities of Greater
and Lesser Helium, duo-capital of Barsoom's greatest existing empire.
The nation of Helium extends from the southern ice fields to and beyond the equator, and from Torquas in the west to the dead city of
Korad in the east. It contains several other great cities, including Hastor in the south, Zor in the southeast, and Zodanga, 5100 haads due
east.

South of Zodanga lies the territory of the Tharks, greatest of the
green tribes of Barsoom. To the east of Thark is the country of the
Warhoons, another green horde and sworn enemies of the Tharks.

Between them but near their northern borders is Barsoom's great
atmosphere plant, without which she would soon become a dead and
airless world. Due north of the plant but still south of the equator is
the deserted city of Korad. Several thousand haads to the northeast
and lying directly on the equator is the famous Kaolian Forest, within
which will be found the metropolis of Kaol, together with several
lesser cities.

The Polar Regions

Barsoom's north polar region is cold, desolate, and snow-covered. It is isolated from the rest of the world by barren granite hills and a mighty ice barrier, which prevent any traffic other than by air. There are two exceptions: first, the Carrion Caves, a former riverbed which breaches the cliff of ice and rock and leads to the land of Okar; second, a narrow corridor through blocks of ice, fallen rocks, and deep snow — the gateway to Panar.

Within this barrier lie two countries, Okar, the home of the yellow-skinned, black-bearded people who dwell in the glass-domed cities of Marentina, Kadabra, Illall, and others; and Panar, a nation of red men living within their hothouse city of Pankor. No record of any intercourse exists between these two states.

The south polar region also shelters two races: the therns, white-skinned priests of Issus, who dwell in and on the Otz Mountains that encircle the south pole; and the black-skinned First Born, who live in a city in the Valley Dor and on an underground sea, the Sea of Omean, which harbors their mighty fleet.

The Lost Sea of Korus, the only existing large body of water on the surface of Barsoom, lies over the south pole, in the center of the lush Valley Dor. Both are entirely surrounded by the towering Otz Mountains, which sprawl northward into the Otz Valley, which, in turn, is surrounded by the southern ice fields. Two miles under these valleys and these mountains is the great subterranean Sea of Omean, secret base of the First Born, and larger even than the Lost Sea of Korus.

As stated earlier, when Mars is at perihelion (closest to the sun) the south polar region experiences its summer season, whereas the northern polar area is in sunlight only when the planet is some twenty-six million miles further away, at aphelion. With these conditions in mind, Burroughs chose to create an eternally frigid, ice-bound region in the north and an area of a semi-tropical nature at the south pole. This southernmost part of Barsoom is a huge basin or pocket containing two bodies of water, the Lost Sea of Korus on the surface and the larger Sea of Omean some two miles below.

It is possible that the five-thousand-foot-high Golden Cliffs, which form the sides of the basin, are of such a nature that they retain the heat received from the sun in the summer and thus maintain the Valley Dor at a semi-tropical temperature during the rest of the Barsoomian year, though there may be snow outside the cliffs and just beyond the Otz Mountains. It is also possible that the Sea of Omean is warmed by internal heat and that, in turn, the soil of the valley and the water of the Lost Sea of Korus receive the benefit of this warmth.

The accompanying maps of Barsoom include two hemispheres. On the left is the western and on the right, the eastern. They differ, however, from comparable maps of Earth for, where we use Long. 0° and 180° to divide our hemispheres, on Barsoom it is the custom to extend 90° both east and west from the Prime Meridian at Exum to create the western hemisphere and the same from Long. 180° to form the eastern hemisphere.

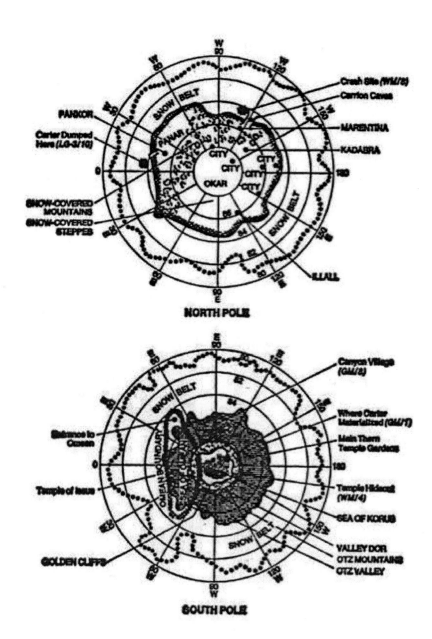

NORTH POLE

SOUTH POLE

Adapted by *Gene Siegel* from a design and graphics by John F. Roy and E. Campbell

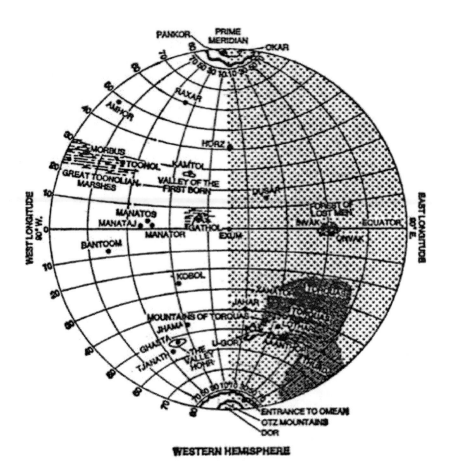

WESTERN HEMISPHERE

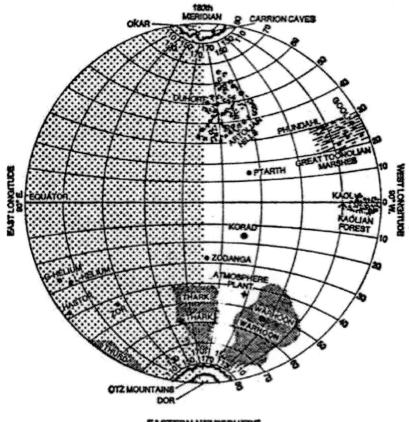

EASTERN HEMISPHERE

Thus, it can be seen that Carthoris was correct when he said (*TMM/3*) that he was indeed in the western hemisphere though he was over the deserted city of Aaanthor which, we are told, is located at approximately Lat. 50° south and Long. 40° east. (*TMM/12*).

Also correct is the statement, "...the three great powers of the eastern hemisphere—Helium, Ptarth, and Kaol" *(TMM/10)*, despite the fact that Helium is, meridianwise, east of Exum, whereas Ptarth and Kaol are to its west.

Given hereunder is a sample of the code of reference used in the following "Gazetteer-Index of Barsoomian Place Names," as well as in the glossaries that follow.

PM/3   =   *A Princess of* Mars/third chapter only

PM/3,7   =   " " " / third and seventh chapters

PM/3-6   =   " " " / third through sixth chapters

PM/3+   =   " " " / third chapter to end of book

PM/-   =   " " " / the entire book

[Note: A chapter of *F'word* indicates a book's Foreword]

Llana of Gathol is made up of four "books." Thus: *LG-2/6* = *Llana of Gathol*, Book 2/Chapter Six only. And so on.

A Gazetteer-Index of Barsoomian Place Names

Aaanthor: {TMM/4,12} One of ancient Barsoom's great seaports, now inhabited only by white apes and roving green men. It lies at Lat. 50° S. and Long. 40° E. The great street that stretches from the waterfront to the central square is still known as the Avenue of Quays, and is lined with empty palaces and old-world monoliths.

Amhor: {MMM/4; SMM/23-27} A city-state some 2000 haads north of the Toonolian Marshes and 5000 haads east of Duhor. The chief business of the state is the raising of thoats and zitidars, the former the saddle animals and the latter the mammoth draft animals of Barsoom. Both are also raised for food, and Amhor exports preserved meats, hides, and other byproducts to Duhor, Phundahl and Toonol. It has a fine zoological garden which, at one time under its jed Jal Had, even placed humans on exhibition.

Artolian Hills: {MMM/4; SMM/2} An extensive range of hills surrounding the city of Duhor. Some of its peaks are snow-covered. It lies between 2000 and 3000 haads north of Ptarth and the same distance west of Phundahl.

Atmosphere Plant: {PM/20; WM/9} The building that contains "the machinery which produces that artificial atmosphere which sustains life on Mars. The secret of the entire process hinges on the use of the ninth ray... There is always sufficient reserve of the ninth ray stored in the great building to maintain the present Martian atmosphere for a thousand years, and the only fear... was that some accident might befall the pumping apparatus... a battery of twenty radium pumps any one of which was equal to the task of furnishing all Mars with the atmosphere compound" *(PM/20)*.

The plant is a huge building, two hundred feet high and covering some four square miles. It has only one entrance, composed of three doors each twenty feet thick and controlled only by a series of thought waves. The walls are one hundred and fifty feet thick and the

roof is made of glass five feet thick. The responsibility for this building rests with two men skilled in their duties, each man serving for
half a year at a stretch.

There is a second, and presumably smaller, atmosphere plant in
Marentina which supplies breathable air to all the domed cities in the
arctic nation of Okar. Whether or not it also augments the outside air
over the polar region is not stated.

Bantoom: {CM/3-9} Land of the kaldanes. A series of fertile valleys
and low hills and — what is most unusual — open streams. It lies south
of the equator and several thousand haads to the west of Gathol.

Barsoom: The planet Mars, as named by its inhabitants.

Carrion Caves: {WM/8} A series of twenty-seven connecting caves
which form the only passage beneath the ice barrier and lead from the
outside world to the arctic land of Okar. A former riverbed, it now
serves as both a charnel-house for the Okarians and a lair for the savage white-furred apts.

Cluros: Barsoomian name for the further moon, known to us as
Deimos.

Cosoom: Barsoomian name for the planet Venus.

Domnia: {SM/20,24} One of the major kingdoms of Ladan, or Thuria. It lies far across the mountains from Tarid, the spot where John
Carter landed on the satellite.

Dor: *see Valley Dor.*

Duhor: {MMM/4,6,14; FMM/F'word; SMM/1,2} A city-state in the
Artolian Hills, some 10,500 haads northeast of Helium. (NOTE: The
confusing statement "northwest of the Twin Cities of Helium," which
appears in Chap. 2 of all book editions of *SMM* is an error. The *Argosy*
magazine version [Jan. 7, 1939] correctly states "northeast.") It is ruled

by its jeddak, Kor San, father of Valla Dia, who married Vad Varo, otherwise known as Ulysses Paxton of the U.S.A.

Dusar: {TMM/-; FMM/16; LG-4/1} A powerful northern nation in Barsoom's western hemisphere whose capital, Dusar, lies at Long. 20° E. and Lat. 15° N. Its domain stretches far to the south, one of its canals passing to the northeast of Torquas. It is noted for its fine honey. Nutus, father of Prince Astok, is jeddak.

Eurobus: The planet Jupiter, in the language of its natives.

Exum: {SMM/2; LG-1/1} A center of unknown size, on the equator at the Prime Meridian. The Barsoomian Greenwich. It may be nothing more than a single building containing scientific equipment — similar to the Atmosphere Plant.

"forbidden land," the: {WM/8} Name used by the Barsoomians of the outer world when speaking of the arctic region beyond the barrier ice cliffs of the north polar area.

Forest of Lost Men, the: {LG-4/-} One of the rare wooded areas of Barsoom. It lies along the equator, roughly on a line from Helium to Dusar. It contains, among other things, skeel, sorapus, and sompus trees. It shelters two cities, Invak and Onvak, that are constantly at war with one another.

Garobus: The planet Mars, in the language of the Jovians.

Gathol: {CM/-; FMM/1; LG/-} A small but wealthy western-hemisphere nation stretching from Lat. 10° N. to the equator and from Long. 10° W. to Long. 20° W. The city of Gathol, thought to be the oldest inhabited city on Barsoom, is built upon a mountain surrounded by a great salt marsh. Beyond this is a fertile plain, to the west of which is a barren land of crags and canyons that are virtually impassable. The mountain, which was formerly an island in the Throxeus Ocean, is famous for its diamond mines. Great herds of thoats and zitidars are raised on the plain. Its jed is Gahan, husband of Tara of Helium and father of Llana of Gathol.

Ghasta: {FMM/7-9} A small walled city deep in the crater of an extinct volcano, on the bank of the River Syl. The crater, known as the Valley Hohr, is forested, and inhabited by huge spiders. The population of Ghasta is only 100 members of the court and 500 slaves. Ghron, its mad jed, delights in torturing and maiming his hapless subjects.

Golden Cliffs, the: {GM/1; WM/1} Five-thousand-foot-high, perpendicular cliffs that surround the Valley Dor. They form the inner border of the Otz Mountains, which ring the south pole of Barsoom. The face of the entire cliffs is shot with veins and patches of solid gold, as well as outcroppings of ruby, emerald, and diamond boulders. The cliffs are honeycombed with caves that stretch deep into the base of the mountains.

Gooli: {SMM/20-22} A village of thatched huts on the island of Ompt, in a lake in the Toonolian Marshes. Its jed is Anatok, and its inhabitants are oviparous marsupials. The Goolians are ignorant, vain, and cowardly.

Great Toonolian Marshes: *see Toonolian Marshes.*

Greater Helium: *see Helium.*

Gulf of Torquas: {FMM/2-3} Now a moss-covered valley. Its waters once stretched from Torquas on the east to Xanator on the west.

Hastor: {FM/18-20; WM/6; FMM/1; SMM/25; LG-3/7} A Heliumatic city noted for its shipbuilding. It lies near the southern border of the nation, some 500 haads south of the Twin Cities, and doubtless serves as a bastion against the savage Thurds.

Helium: {PM to JCM(SMJ)} The greatest nation on present-day Barsoom. Its boundaries extend from the southern ice fields, where water is obtained for its canals, to and beyond the equator; and from the borders of Torquas in the west to an undefined frontier far to the east. Strongly guarded farms border the vital canals, their crops and herds eventually finding their way to the numerous cities scattered across the nation. Various "dead cities," those magnificent monuments to a long-dead past, lie within the boundaries of Helium, as does the great Atmosphere Plant, without which all Barsoom would perish.

Almost always at war, either with a neighbor, or with one of the many green tribes, Helium has built up the most formidable navy on Barsoom. This same navy also turns its skills to such duties as charting the air currents and taking atmospheric density tests, this being necessary in the maintenance of the air supply for the entire world at its essential level.

Within the borders of the empire are several dry seabeds, ranges of modest mountains, miles of rolling hills, and here and there, valleys whose soil still holds enough moisture to support small forests, the commercial value of which cannot be overestimated. Mining is fairly extensive in the hills and plateaus; gold, platinum, diamonds, semi-precious stones, and even oil are taken from the soil. There are also great quarries of marble and granite, which supply the material for the great buildings and the city walls.

The capital of the Heliumatic Empire is unique in that it consists of two immense, circular, walled cities, some seventy-five miles apart. They can be identified by two lofty towers — one of vivid scarlet, rising nearly a mile into the air from the center of Greater Helium, while the other, of bright yellow and the same height, marks her sister, Lesser Helium. The two centers are connected by an underground system, with great pneumatic stations at each end. Automatic carriers travel from one metropolis to the other with the speed of a bullet. The two cities (in the eastern hemisphere) lie on a broad plain near the 30th parallel South, between Long. 110° and 100° East.

Tardos Mors, Jeddak of Helium, rules his empire from Greater Helium, and his son, Mors Kajak, is Jed of Lesser Helium. John Carter, Prince of Helium and Warlord of Barsoom, maintains a palace in each city.

The main entrance to Greater Helium is the Gate of Jeddaks. It opens onto the broad, moss-cushioned Avenue of Ancestors, which stretches for five miles into the heart of the city, terminating in a huge plaza fronting the great Temple of Reward. It is in this magnificent edifice that heros are honored, savants rewarded, and criminals and traitors punished. Such individuals are led up the wide Aisle of Hope to the Pedestal of Truth, where they stand before the Throne of Righteousness; and here they are judged.

Enormous buildings house Helium's fighting men, and the roofs of these barracks are the aerial docks for the mighty Heliumatic fleet. Other structures serve as terminals for freighters, and still others for passenger craft.

Private homes are built with slender metal columns upon which they are raised into the air at night, mainly to avoid assassins. In some instances, only the sleeping chambers are thus elevated. Not so, however, with the more wealthy classes, who can afford their own private guards. Here will be found palatial buildings with carven balconies, and flat roofs furnished with couches and canopies. The spacious grounds contain flower gardens, ferns, shrubs of pimalia and sorapus, and marble statuary. Paths graveled with brilliant semiprecious stones wind through the scarlet sward. Inside such a residence may be found beautifully appointed corridors and ramps leading to a ballroom, a library, reception rooms, a dining hall, and—on the upper levels—the bedrooms and private suites. The bath will contain a pool of scented water in a marble basin, while overhead a glass dome lets in the sunlight. Both servants and slaves will be busy with the many household tasks.

Hohr, the Valley: {FMM/7} This tropical and fertile valley, not too far from Tjanath, was formed by the River Syl flowing across the crater of a gigantic and long-extinct volcano. Hemmed in by mighty cliffs and located in a rocky and barren part of Barsoom, this remnant of an ancient era is a haven of trees, flowers, shrubs, fruit, birds, and insects of both a prehistoric and a modern world. In its center is the gloomy castle of Ghasta.

Holy Land, the: {GM/8} A title sometimes used by the Black Pirates when referring to the Valley Dor, site of the Temple of Issus.

Horz: {TMM/12; LG-1/-; LG-2/1; LG-4/1} Capital city of Barsoom's greatest nation of a million years ago. At that time it was the seat of learning and culture of the then-dominant white-skinned Orovars. It is thought to have been the point from which the longitude and latitude of Barsoom was calculated in that era.

Illall: {WM/9} One of the domed cities of Okar, and the most remote from Kadabra, its capital.

Invak: {LG-4/-} A city in the Forest of Lost Men, which lies in a long, deep valley directly over the equator, some 5000 haads east of Gathol. Its people have developed a pill which, when taken, makes them invisible for about a day. Their jeddak is Ptantus.

Iss, the River: {PM/24; GM/-; WM/1-7} Also known as the River of Death or River of Mystery. It is said to flow the length of Barsoom, presumably underground, passing under the Otz Mountains and emptying into the Lost Sea of Korus in the Valley Dor. Although its course is not given in any of the chronicles, we are told there are various access points where boats can be had for those wishing to take the final pilgrimage to the Barsoomian Elysium.

Jahar: {FMM/-} A nation of red men to the west of the Mountains of Torquas. Its late jeddak, Tul Axtar, was best known for his harem of beautiful women, said to number in the thousands. Its southern province, U-Gor, once a rich agricultural district, now lies denuded due to extreme overpopulation demanded by Tul Axtar in his mad desire to strengthen his nation.

Jasoom: Barsoomian name for Earth.

Jhama: {FMM/9+} An ancient, isolated castle to the northeast of Tjanath and west of Jahar. It was more recently occupied by the Jaharian scientist, Phor Tak, inventor of the Flying Death.

Kadabra: {WM/9+} The capital city of Okar, the arctic nation of yellow men. A large, glass-domed metropolis having a circumference of one hundred miles, and located adjacent to the north magnetic pole.

Kamtol: {LG-2/-} A city of the Black Pirates, in the Valley of the First Born. A beautiful city of some 200,000 population, with elaborately carved, pure white walls, broad avenues, and graceful, lofty towers.

Kaol: (a) {WM/5-7,16; TMM/10,13,14} A small but powerful empire of red men, seated on the equator almost halfway around the planet to the east of Helium. Lying, as it does, in a natural depression, climatic conditions are such that the entire area is heavily forested, an unusual feature on this dying planet. Isolated and entirely self-supporting, its people are deeply loyal to both state and doctrine. Its jeddak is Kulan Tith.

There are several cities within the Kaolian Forest, connected by a splendid network of roads. When John Carter first visited this country, Kaol had no aircraft and therefore no landing areas. However, since then they have acquired a respectable armada.

Kaol: (b) {WM/5-7,16} The capital city of the empire of Kaol. It is completely encircled by a seventy-five-foot-high wall, smooth as glass, and has a slender watchtower rising above the surrounding trees.

Kaolian Forest: *see Kaol (a).*

Kobol: {FMM/1,16; LG-3/4} A little-known city-state somewhere in the western portion of the southern hemisphere, likely not too far north of Jhama and Tjanath. Ruled by a jed, it was sacked by Helium fourteen years prior to the "Tul Axtar Incident."

Korad: {PM/4,11,12} One of the greatest of the pre-drought cities of Barsoom. Long deserted, except for roving bands of green men, it was once a busy seaport. Bordering its central plaza is a magnificent structure of white marble inlaid with gold and brilliant stones, and with a canopied entrance one hundred feet in width. Its inner walls are decorated with beautiful mural paintings and mosaics, scenes of the earlier Barsoom. Its gardens still contain fountains, statuary, benches, and pergola-like contraptions. Korad lies just south of the equator, to the east of Zodanga and roughly on a line with it and Helium.

Korus, the Lost Sea of: {PM/11; GM/-; WM/1,16; TMM/4; LG-2/3} The only large body of water left on the surface of Barsoom. Located at the south pole, it occupies most of the Valley Dor and is completely surrounded by the towering, ice-capped Otz Mountains. The River Iss drains into the Sea of Korus through a passage worn under the Golden Cliffs. In turn, Korus pours its waters into the larger, underground Sea of Omean.

Ladan: {SM/18,19} Name given by its inhabitants to Thuria, the nearer moon of Barsoom.

Land of Lost Souls, the: {GM/8,20} A narrow band of fertile and well-watered land at the outer base of the Otz Mountains. Cut off from the outside world by the great ice field that encircles the south polar region, it has become the inescapable home of those unfortunate souls who became apprehensive and decided not to enter the Valley Dor — together with slaves who fled from the therns.

Lesser Helium: *see Helium.*

Lost Sea of Korus: *see Korus, the Lost Sea of.*

Lothar: (a) {TMM/5-10} One of the great seaports of ancient Barsoom, and home of the mightiest fleet ever to sail the Throxeus and her four sister oceans. Its location is not given in any of the chronicles.

Lothar: (b) {TMM/5-10} A walled city in an enclosed valley deep in the Mountains of Torquas. When the oceans were evaporating, the pacifist Lotharians fled in panic before the onslaught of the savage green hordes. Millions died, including all the women, in their terrible trek across half a world. Only 20,000 men lived to reach the hidden valley and build their new Lothar. Today only a few hundred are left, under their jeddak, Tario.

Manataj: {CM/16} One of the three principal cities of the nation of Manator, and farthest from its capital.

Manator: (a) {CM/10+} A nation lying to the west of Gathol. Between the two is a country of torn rocks, yawning chasms, and treacherous air currents. Isolated from the rest of Barsoom, Manator has remained in the past, having neither firearms nor aircraft. It is famed for its Jetan Fields, where the game is played with living pieces. Its current jeddak is A-Kor.

Manator: (b) {CM/13+} The capital city of Manator, noted for its great Hall of Chiefs in the jeddak's palace.

Here the embalmed bodies of the departed jeds and jeddaks are arrayed in their battle dress, and here the reigning jeddak holds consultation with them.

Manatos: {CM/13+} The second-most-important city of Manator. It is ruled by U-Thor, who is known as the Great Jed.

Marentina: {WM/9,16} A principality of Okar. Self-supporting and isolated by mountain ranges from the rest of the kingdom, its jed, Talu, rebelled against his jeddak and eventually became ruler of the yellow race. Marentina maintains an atmosphere plant which supplies all Okarian cities with life-giving, breathable air, thus ensuring this arctic nation its independence from the rest of Barsoom.

Masena, country of the: {SM/18,24} Actually more a tribe than a country. These tree-dwelling cat-men live in the forest of Ladan, or Thuria, a day or two traveling time from the castle of the Tarids.

Morbus: {SMM/-} Once a city of the ancients, it was rebuilt by Ras Thavas, the Master Mind of Mars, as a laboratory for experiments in creating synthetic human life. Situated on an island halfway along the northern edge of the Great Toonolian Marshes and some 1900 haads south of Amhor, it was totally destroyed by firebombs from the Heliumatic fleet.

Morgor City: {JCM(SMJ)/3} The capital city of the Morgors, or Skeleton Men, of Jupiter. It is a large metropolis, covering some four hundred square miles, and is completely walled. It is a drab-looking place built of volcanic rock; and all buildings, walls, and pavement are of a uniform dark brown. There are no gardens, no trees or shrubs, and no lawns. "The city was perfectly rectangular, having a long axis of about twenty-five miles and a width of about sixteen. The avenues were perfectly straight and equidistant, one from the other, cutting the city into innumerable, identical square blocks. The buildings were all perfect rectangles, though not all of either the same size or height—the only break in the depressing monotony of this gloomy city" (JCM[SMJ]/3).

Mountains of Torquas: {TMM/4} A sprawling mountain range in the land of the Torquas, a southern green horde, and lying to the northwest of the deserted city of Aaanthor.

Okar: {WM/9+; LG-1/10; LG-3/11} Land of the yellow men of Barsoom. It occupies most of the north Polar region, and is isolated from the outside world by a mighty ice barrier that encircles the frigid zone. It is divided into provinces or principalities, each with a great glass-covered city—Kadabra, Marentina, and Illall being but three. The tyrannical Salensus Oll was jeddak until slain by John Carter, following which Talu, Prince of Marentina, accepted the throne. Okar has its own atmosphere plant, located in the city of Marentina.

Ombra: {SM/24} A country, or nation on Thuria, the nearer moon of Barsoom.

Omean, the Sea of: {GM/8-13,20,21} A subterranean ocean some five or haads beneath a large portion of the south polar area. The main source of its water is the Sea of Korus, which lies, in part, above it. It is the sanctuary for the Black Pirates and harbors their entire fleet with ease. Entrance to this underground sea is through the funnel, some five haads in width, of a long-extinct volcano deep within the polar ice cap. There are also man-made passages from the shore to the Temple of Issus. The sea contains many islands, one of which, the Isle of Shador, serves as a prison. This tremendous cavern receives its light from a phosphorescence in the rock itself.

Ompt: {SMM/20} An island in the Toonolian Marshes, between Morbus and Phundahl, inhabited by a tribe of marsupial humans. Its capital is Gooli, and its jed, Anatok.

Onvak: {LG-4/4} A city in the Forest of Lost Men. Its people are in a constant state of war with the city of Invak.

Otz Mountains: {GM/3-5,8; WM/2,4} A mighty range encircling the Valley Dor and the Lost Sea of Korus. Its inner border, known as the Golden Cliffs, rises vertically from the floor of the Valley Dor, towering in places to a height of five thousand feet. Its outer edges slope away into foothills and on down to the Otz Valley. They are strongly fortified by the therns, who live both on the slopes and within a maze of caves and tunnels.

Otz Valley: {GM/8,20} A tremendous depression taking in almost the entire polar region, and including the Otz Mountains, which start to rise a hundred miles from its outer edge, as well as the Valley Dor and the Lost Sea of Korus. Colloquially speaking, it refers only to the doughnut-shaped depression between the ice fields and the outer Otz Mountain slopes. It is also known as the Land of Lost Souls or the Valley of Lost Souls. The River Iss has cut a deep canyon across this valley, and irresolute pilgrims on their way to Dor have climbed the canyon wall and sought sanctuary in the valley, from which there is no return.

John Carter saw the value of the well-watered area with its "many broad acres that needed no irrigation to bear rich harvests" (*GM/20*).

Panar: {LG-1/10,11; LG-3/6+; LG-4/13} A segment of land adjacent to Okar, in the norther ice cap of Barsoom. Inhabited by red men who dwell in a great domed city called Pankor, they were until recently virtually unknown to the rest of the world. The Jeddak of Panar, Hin Abtol, had found a method of holding men in cold storage for release at a later date. After preserving a million men, he intended thawing them out to form an army and conquer all Barsoom. Unfortunately for him, John Carter and the Heliumatic fleet intervened.

Pankor: {LG-3/4+} The capital city of Panar. A glass-covered metropolis considerably smaller than Kadabra, the capital of neighboring Okar. Beneath the great dome is warmth and comfort. The streets are of moss-like vegetation and the lawns are of crimson grass. The unique, northern-style ground fliers speed along broad avenues. At one time, just outside the city, in the biting arctic cold, were stored the frozen bodies of thousands of Hin Abtol's troops, awaiting their turn to be restored to life.

Phundahl: {MMM/2,4,6,7,9+; SMM/1,2,4,29,31} A city-state on the western extremity of the Great Toonolian Marshes. Its people, self-centered and aloof, have little intercourse with other nations. Phundahlians worship the god Tur, rather than Issus (the goddess of most Barsoomians until she was exposed by John Carter). The temples of Tur are filled with assorted statuary, each depicting their god in a different form. The powerful priesthood rule their subjects with fear and the suppression of learning. Xaxa was jeddara and High Priestess until she went mad and died; she was succeeded by Dar Tarus as jeddak and High Priest.

Polodona: A Barsoomian word meaning "equator."

Ptarth: (a) {GM/18; WM/7,16; TMM/-; FMM/16} Possibly the second-most-powerful nation on Barsoom. Its borders stretch from the Artolian Hills east to the Toonolian Marshes, south to the equator, east to the boundaries of Kaol, and west to the canals of Duhor. Its jeddak is Thuvan Dihn, father of Thuvia of Ptarth. Ptarth is famous for its fine wines.

Ptarth: (b) {see above} The capital city of Ptarth. It lies 9500 haads northeast of Helium and at a point south of and equidistant from Duhor and Phundahl.

Rasoom: The Barsoomian name for the planet Mercury.

Raxar: {LG-3/7} A small nation of red men, presumably in the western hemisphere and to the north of Gathol. Hin Abtol, Jeddak of Panar, sacked its capital on his way from Panar to Gathol.

River Iss, the: *see Iss, the River.*

River of Death: A name sometimes applied to the River Iss. *See Iss, the River.*

River of Mystery: Another name for the River Iss. *See Iss, the River.*

River, Syl, the: *see Syl, the River.*

Sasoom: The Barsoomian name for the planet Jupiter.

Shador: {GM/9-13} An island near the north shore of the Sea of Omean. The First Born use it as a prison.

Syl, the River: {FMM/7; CM/12} A great underground stream flowing far beneath the city of Tjanath and through the Valley Hohr. Very likely a tributary of the River Iss, and possibly the same stream that flows beneath the city of Manator.

Tarid: {SM/16-23} Once a powerful nation on Thuria, or Ladan as the natives call it. Now its citizens number only a thousand or so, and their territory consists of one walled castle on the banks of a river. They are sun-worshippers, and their jeddak, Ul Vas, is known as The All-Highest.

Thark: (a) {PM/7,16} Territory ruled by a green tribe of the same name: "...an enormous tract of arid and semi-arid land between forty and eighty degrees south latitude, and bounded on the east and west by two large fertile tracts" (PM/7). It lies well to the southeast of the Twin Cities of Helium. Its population of some thirty thousand is divided into twenty-five communities, five of which dwell in the city of

Thark and the remainder of which are scattered among other deserted cities within their domain.

Thark: (b) {PM/7,16} Once one of ancient Barsoom's greatest seaports, lying deep in the southern portion of the eastern hemisphere. It is now the headquarters of the most powerful of the green tribes, and from it they take their name.

Throxeus (or Throxus): {LG-1/9,12; CM/1; LG-1/9-12; LG-3/1} Mightiest of the five oceans of Barsoom, and the only one to be named in the chronicles. Its actual location and size are not known, but it covered much of the northern hemisphere from Horz to the equator, and possibly as far east as the Artolian Hills. The swamplands of Gathol are all that remain of this once-great body of water.

Thurd: {TMM/11} That district controlled by a green tribe of the same name. It is located in the southeastern portion of the western hemisphere and spreads over into the eastern hemisphere.

Thuria: Barsoomian name for Phobos, the nearer moon of Mars.

Tjanath: {FMM/2,4-7,10,13,17} A city in the southern part of the western hemisphere. Its jed is Haj Osis. It is noted for "The Death," a unique method of execution where the prisoner is lowered into a pit beneath the palace; even the jed himself has no idea what fate awaits the victim therein.

Toonol: {MMM/2,4,6-9,13,14; SMM/1,4,9,15,16,24} A city-state situated at the eastern end of the Great Toonolian Marshes. Its jeddak is Vobis Kan. It was, until recently, the home Ras Thavas, the Master Mind of Mars, Although aloof from the rest of Barsoom, Toonol has most of the modern features, including a navy, one-man equilibrimotors, shadowless streetlights, and houses that rise on metal shafts. The Toonolians also have astronomical cameras, capable of taking detailed pictures of Earth. Toonolians are a philosophical people, truthful, atheistic, and highly scientific.

Toonolian Marshes, the Great: {MMM/6; SMM/1,4,14,15,19-23,28-31} This last great remnant oceans that once covered much of the surface of Barsoom stretches east and west for 500 haads, across the northern part of the globe, with a maximum width of 800 haads. The land is marshy, with the occasional rocky island supporting a bit of jungle growth. Narrow water channels and small lakes are scattered throughout the area. Savage beasts and water-dwelling reptiles inhabit the swamps, as do tribes of aborigines — or more probably, degenerates — isolated from the civilized world.

At its eastern extremity lies the city of Toonol, and at its western, the city of Phundahl. About midway along its northern edge was the small city of Morbus, now destroyed. On the island of Ompt, within the swamp, is the village of Gooli.

Torquas: (a) {TMM/4-12; FMM/2-5} That area controlled by the green Torquasians under their jeddak, Hortan Gur. It stretches from Xanator and Torquas in the north to Aaanthor and the land of the Thurds in the south, and embraces the eastern foothills of the Mountains of Torquas.

Torquas: (b) {CM/2; FMM/2} One of the most magnificent of the deserted cities of the ancients, now used as headquarters for a tribe of green men, known as Torquasians. It lies roughly 7000 haads west of Helium.

Twin Cities of Helium: *see Helium.*

U-Gor: {FMM/14-15} A province of Jahar. It was once a rich agricultural area, but due to Tul Axtar's mad desire for manpower it became vastly overpopulated. Soon every growing thing was eaten and its people became cannibals. It is now a wasteland.

Valley Dor, the: {PM/11; GM/-; WM/1-7,16; LG-2/4,10-12} A fertile valley at the south pole of Barsoom, entirely surrounded by the towering inner cliffs of the Otz Mountains. In its center lies the Lost Sea of Korus, fed by the River Iss. Here also will be found the Golden Temple of Issus, home of the blackskinned First Born.

This enormous crater-like basin has a tropical climate, with a summer twice as long as Earth's, during which time, due to the tilt of the planet's axis, the sun is almost directly overhead. The valley is covered with crimson grass-like vegetation and contains groves of magnificent trees, some stretching upward for a thousand feet and more, and with trunks a hundred feet in diameter. It is inhabited by the hideous plant men, the great white apes, and brilliant, voiceless birds. Until John Carter exposed the false religion of both the First Born and the white-skinned therns, Valley Dor was believed to be Heaven itself, and was voluntarily sought by countless Barsoomian.

Valley of the First Born, the: {LG-2/-} A long chasm, some two miles deep and ten miles wide, 2500 haads southwest of Horz and almost due north of Gathol. Presumably it was a "deep" in the bottom of the now-dry Throxeus Ocean. It contains several small rivers and a lake, and is well forested. Its inhabitants are a branch of the black-skinned First Born, under their jeddak, Doxus. The capital is Kamtol.

Valley Hohr, the: *see Hohr, the Valley.*

Valley of Lost Souls, the: *see Land of Lost Souls, the.*

Warhoon: (a) {PM/18,19; GM/14,15; WM/7} The land of the Warhoons, one of the savage tribes of green men, and deadly enemies of the Tharks. This tribe is divided into the Warhoons of the North, under their jeddak, Dak Kova, and the Warhoons of the South, under Kab Kadja.

Warhoon: (b) {PM/18,19,24} One of the dead cities of Barsoom, deep in the southern hemisphere to the east of Thark and southeast of the Atmosphere Plant.

Xanator: {FMM/3-5} Once a great seaport on the west coast of the Gulf of Torquas, it is now another deserted city, a stopover for wandering green men. Two thousand haads to the east, on the opposite shore of the now-dry gulf, was the rival port of Torquas.

Zanor: {JCM(SMJ)/5,8,9} An island on the planet Sasoom, or Jupiter, and home of the blue-skinned Savators. A small, rugged country with mountains twenty miles high.

Zodanga: (a) {PM/19-26, GM/16-20} Formerly a mighty kingdom lying 2700 haads to the east of Helium, stretching north to the equator and south to Thark. It is now part of the empire of Helium. Jeddak, until its defeat by John Carter, was Than Kosis. Helium then appointed Zat Arrras as jed.

Zodanga: (b) {PM/19-26; GM/16-20; SM/-} The capital city of the nation of Zodanga, and nearest center to the Atmosphere Plant so vital to all Barsoom. The city walls are seventy-five feet in height, fifty feet thick, and constructed of enormous blocks of carborundum. The central plaza covers a square mile and is bounded by the palaces of the jeddak, the jeds, and other members of the royalty and nobility of Zodanga, as well as by the principal public buildings, cafes, and shops. The city was almost completely gutted by those green hordes temporarily allied with John Carter during his first year on Barsoom, but was later restored to its former magnificence.

(NOTE: Students of the canon have expressed dismay over the statement in Chap. 23 of *A Princess of Mars*, which says, "Helium lies a thousand miles southwest of Zodanga," and one found in Chap. 1 of *Swords of Mars*, "Over nineteen hundred miles east of The Twin Cities of Helium, at about Lat. 30° S., Lon. 172° E., lies Zodanga."

Of the various solutions offered for this seeming contradiction, I feel the most logical is the one put forth by the late Frank J. Brueckel, in *Barsoomian* [#13], dated January, 1968. He suggested that Carter's belief—in *A Princess of Mars*—that Zodanga was a thousand miles northeast of Helium was due to the unimportance of its locality at the time he was being given a short course in Barsoomian geography by Dejah Thoris. The only thing of importance then was how to get from Thark to Helium. It is likely that she meant that it was a thousand miles from Helium to the *borders* of the nation of Zodanga, and there would be no reason for her to tell him that the two *cities* were nineteen hundred miles apart.)

Zor: {JCM(SMJ)/1,2} A small city-state slightly over 1000 haads southeast of the Twin Cities of Helium. Formerly an enemy, it was recently conquered by and made part of the Heliumatic Empire. Presumably this was one of the cities once referred to by Dejah Thoris as being "not friendly toward Helium" (PM/16).

Chapter III – A Biography of Barsoom, Including a Dictionary of People, Past and Present, Whose Names Appear in the Barsoomian Sagas

As all Barsoomians are aware, life on their planet started with the Tree of Life some twenty-three million years ago. For century after countless century this Tree, which grew in the heart of the Valley Dor, produced fruit that eventually developed into tiny plant men still attached to its branches and three other sections — "pods" — which fell to the ground. These three fallen pods — each containing a living, reasoning being — hopped, rolled, and floated over the entire surface of Barsoom. In time, one of the pod-enclosed creatures burst its shell and emerged into the sunlight. He then broke open other shells and the population explosion began (GM/7).

This first entity was a black man and his strain has remained unsullied to the present day — in the form of the First Born, or the Black Pirates. From the two other kinds of pods came the multi-legged worm and the white ape. These two creatures — plus early, "renegade" blacks — were the source of all animal life on Barsoom. Age after age of evolution went by before the white-skinned and the yellow-skinned tribes of men developed — those we now know as Orovars and Okarians. It wasn't until after the oceans dried up, a mere half-million years ago, that the now-predominant red man came into existence — the result of the blending of survivors of all these branches of the human race.

The black race — or First Born, as they call themselves — are a proud people. The men stand six feet and more in height. They have fine, regular features; their skin is like polished ebony; the iris of their eyes is black and set in clear white eyeballs. They are a grim, bloodthirsty race, with an unquenchable desire to fight and an aversion for work. This last no doubt explains why they did not become the paramount race of Barsoom. There is some suggestion that at one time the First Born had a language of their own; that is to say, it differed from the otherwise universal language of the rest of Barsoom. But that difference, if it existed, seems to have been lost over the ages. Only a few words unique to their race now remain in use by the blacks (see *PM/11* and *WM/8*).

The white-skinned race — the Orovars — were the most progressive. As time went on, they spread across the land, tilling the soil, taming beasts of burden, building cities and molding nations, constructing ships and conquering the oceans. For many thousands of years they were the dominant, highly civilized masters of the world. The now-deserted but still-magnificent cities of Horz, Korad, and Aaanthor still stand as perpetual monuments to their supremacy.

They were a fair-skinned, auburn- or yellow-haired race — peace-loving, creative, and industrious. With the exception of two small groups — the etherealistic Lotharians and the stubborn hidden citizens of ancient Horz — the Orovars have disappeared from the face of Barsoom.

There is, however, an offshoot of the white-skinned race: the therns. Strongly entrenched in the bowels of the Otz Mountains, at the south pole, this arrogant cult chose to consider themselves demigods, servants of Issus, the Goddess of Eternal Life; and they made themselves priests and guardians of all Barsoom. The therns are a bald race and have been so for many generations, but since they consider this to be a stigma, they consequently all wear wigs of flowing blond locks to more resemble their ancient forebears.

Little is known of the history of the yellow-skinned race. Apparently they inhabited the northern part of Barsoom and as the oceans receded they withdrew behind the polar ice cap, where they devised ways to combat the weather and climatic conditions, chiefly by means of glass-domed hothouse cities. What physical changes, if any, took place over the centuries we do not know, but today their skins are the color of ripe lemons, their hair is black, and the men are heavily bearded.

The green men of Barsoom are a race apart. Their climb up the ladder of evolution followed a different path from that of the biped First Born, Orovar, and Okarian. Olive-skinned, hairless, six-limbed, with protruding and independently-working eyes, antenna-like ears, tusks, and an almost complete lack of human emotions, they suggest an origin more reptilian than human. Their size—twelve to fifteen feet in height—their hatred for all other members of the human race (including all other green tribes), and their cruelty and lust for battle make them the most feared creatures on Barsoom. Imagine the horror and panic felt by the civilized races as the seas dried up and the towering four-armed savages—not seamen—no longer confined by ocean barriers, stormed across a hapless planet.

The principal race upon Barsoom today is the red man, who differs but little in physical appearance from Earth man. The fact that his skin is a light-reddish copper color and the female is oviparous constitute the two most marked divergences from Anglo-Saxon standards. Except for one other: his longevity. A thousand years is the natural span of life of a red Martian, although because of war-like activities and the prevalence of assassination, few live their allotted span. The red men's hair is uniformly black, and the males are beardless.

The red man's general political organization has changed little over the countless ages, the primary unit still being the tribe, at the head of which is a chief, or jed, corresponding in modern Earth times to king. The princes are known as lesser jeds, while the chief of chiefs, or the head of consolidated tribes, is the jeddak, or emperor, whose consort is a jeddara.

The majority of red Martians live in walled cities, though many reside in isolated, though well-walled and-defended, farm homes along those rich irrigated ribbons of land that we of Earth know as the Canals of Mars.

The military forces of the red men are highly organized, the principal arm of the service being the navy, an enormous air force of battleships, cruisers, and an infinite variety of lesser craft down to one-man scout fliers. Next in size and importance is the infantry branch of the service; while the cavalry, mounted on a breed of small thoats, is utilized principally in patrolling the avenues of the cities and the rural districts that border the irrigating systems.

Science, literature, art, and architecture are in some ways further advanced upon the planet than upon Earth—a remarkable thing when one considers that constant battle for survival is the most marked characteristic of life upon Barsoom. Furthermore, notwithstanding all the grim realities with which they have to contend, the red Martians are a happy, social people. They have their games, their dances, and their songs, and the social life of a great capital of Barsoom is as gay and magnificent as any that may be found in the rich capitals of Earth.

(The above description is almost verbatim from the Foreword to *A Fighting Man of Mars*—for who could say it better than Edgar Rice Burroughs himself.)

In this same vein, may I refer the reader to the second half of Chapter 2 of *Thuvia, Maid of Mars* for an excellent and detailed description of the activity seen on the streets of Helium in the course of a single day: the tradesman on his way to work, the woman at home, the traffic on the avenues, the scene in the public slave market. Chapter 1 of *The Chessmen of Mars* takes us on a tour of the Warlord's palace in Greater Helium, and to a state ball. The first half of Chapter 9 of *The Master Mind of Mars* paints a fine picture of the house of a nobleman in the city of Toonol, and shows how far advanced Barsoomians are in the fields of astronomical instruments, wireless photography, and wireless telephony.

Two minor offshoots of mankind upon Barsoom are the kaldanes of Bantoom and the marsupials of the Toonolian swamplands.

The kaldanes are a race of bodiless heads with six spider-like legs and two stout chelae, or claws. They live in underground cells and passageways, coming to the surface only for essentials such as the gathering of food. They are sexless, except for the king, who is bisexual and oviparous. Every thousandth egg is a king egg and is either destroyed or stored away, to be hatched only if the ruling king dies. Kaldanes consider the brain is everything, and eventually hope to reach the stage where—deaf, dumb, and blind—they can merely sit and think, needing neither air nor food. Already they have only the simplest of vital organs, and do not breathe as they have no lungs.

For transportation, other than in their burrows, they have developed the rykor. Formerly a fourlegged, burrowing animal which they rode, it has been trained to walk erect and then crossed with captive red men to eventually become a headless humanoid creature upon whose shoulders the kaldanes sit and direct its muscles and nervous system by attaching their tentacles to its spine.

Deep within the Great Toonolian Marshes are a race of oviparous marsupials. These creatures have long, powerful legs and large, muscular tails; otherwise they are quite human. They move in prodigious leaps, much like a kangaroo of Earth. The females have a pouch in which they place their egg. Here it hatches and here the young shelters itself until able to fend for itself. Although quite primitive, these marsupials possess swords, knives, and spears and live in thatched huts. They speak the universal language of Barsoom.

The hormads, created by Ras Thavas, the Master Mind of Mars, represented, for a few short years, an artificial or synthetic branch of humanity on Barsoom. After being expelled from his estate near Toonol, Ras Thavas set up a laboratory in the abandoned city of Morbus on an island in the Great Toonolian Marshes in order to further his experiment, that of creating "human beings from human tissue" (SMM/4). He succeeded, disastrously. Most hormads proved to be of low intelligence, but some developed normal brains. This latter group rebelled against the scientist and forced him to increase the rate of their production in order that they might conquer all Barsoom. It was only through the intervention of John Carter and the Heliumatic fleet that these quasi-human creatures were completely eliminated before their aims could be carried out.

While on Thuria, the nearer moon of Barsoom, Carter encountered tribes of white-skinned people with blue hair, who appear to be the dominant race on Ladan, as they call it.

The only other type of human he met on Thuria were the Masena, a tree-dwelling tribe of people with feline characteristics. While of general human conformation they have but one eye, in the center of the forehead. The pupil is a vertical slit, as in a cat's eye. The ears are small orifices, and the nose is broad and flat. They have two mouths, one above the other. The lower and larger mouth is lipless thus exposing the powerful teeth in a permanent death-like grin. The upper mouth is round, with protruding lips, and is toothless. Their fingers and the four toes of each foot are much longer than the normal human digits, whereas the thumbs and big toes are short and extend at right angles from the hands and feet. They have a stiff yellowish mane, but their most peculiar feature is their ability to change color to match their background, much as an Earthly chameleon.

On Sasoom — or Jupiter, as we know it — Carter came in contact with two types of humans.

The Morgors, who abducted him from Barsoom, are a thin-framed race with parchment-like skin through which their bones can easily be seen. They have solid brown eyes, no lips or nose or external ears, and they are hairless. A cold, merciless, loveless people, they have conquered most of their own world and would now like to seize and control the planet Barsoom.

Another Jovian race, still fighting for existence and freedom in the remote mountain areas, are the Savators. Except for their blue skin, they differ little from the normal humans of Barsoom or Earth.

In the following "Dictionary of People, Past and Present," I have tried to touch on the main point of involvement of each subject, thus drawing the interest of the reader to more than a mere name and occupation.

A Dictionary of People, Past and Present

A-Kor: {CM/11-22} Prince of Manator. The illegitimate son of O-Tar, Jeddak of Manator, and Haja, a princess of Gathol enslaved by the Manatorians. Following the death of O-Tar by his own hand, A-Kor became Jeddak of Manator.

Anatok: {SMM/20-22} Jed of Gooli. Leader of a village of human marsupials situated on an island, Ompt, in the Great Toonolian Marshes. A vain and cowardly fellow.

A-Sor: {CM/18,20} An under-padwar in the guard of O-Tar, Jeddak of Manator. Actually he was Tasor, son of a Gatholian nobleman.

Captured by soldiers from Manataj, he was sold to a princess of that city, who later married him.

Astok: {TMM/1,3,11+} Prince of Dusar. Son of the jeddak, Nutus, and a slave woman. Rebuffed by Thuvia of Ptarth, he had her kidnapped and the blame directed toward Carthoris of Helium. The plot was exposed, but no indication of his fate is contained in the canon.

Ay-mad: {SMM/5,10-20} Name taken by the Third Jed of Morbus when he declared himself jeddak. It means One-Man, or Number-One Man, or First Man. He was one of seven hormads whose brains developed normally and who wrested control of Morbus from Ras Thavas, the Master Mind of Mars.

Bal Tab: {SMM/26-28} A green man captured by Amhorians and placed on exhibit in their great zoo. He was killed while attempting to escape, but not before slaying Jal Had, Prince of Amhor.

Bal Zak: {MMM/7,8} A Toonolian. Captain of the aircraft of Ras Thavas, Master Mind of Mars. He assisted Vad Varo and his companions to escape from the Tower of Thavas.

Bandolian: {JCM(SMJ)/3-7} Emperor of the Morgors, the Skeleton Men of Jupiter. It was his intention to invade and conquer Barsoom. He was a ruthless tyrant and considered all other races to be inferior beings.

Ban-Tor: {LG-2/7-9} A black-skinned First Born soldier in the city of Kamtol. He was bested by John Carter in a duel, branded, and disgraced.

Bar Comas: {PM/18} Jeddak of the Warhoons, a tribe of green men, hereditary enemies of the Tharks. He was killed in hand-to-hand combat by his lieutenant, Dak Kova, who then became jeddak.

Carter, John: {PM to JCM(SMJ)} Earthman, Virginian, Prince of Helium, Warlord of Mars, the greatest swordsman of two worlds. No one, not even this living enigma himself, knows when or where he was born. In speaking of his age, Carter says, "I am a very old man; how old I do not know. Possibly I am a hundred, possibly more; but I cannot tell because I have never aged as other men, nor do I remember any childhood. So far as I can recollect I have always been a man, a man of about thirty" (PM/1). From the meager information available, I gather that Carter was born in Virginia — or brought there as an infant — in the early part of the eighteenth century. At the time of his first "death" on Earth, in March, 1866, he could have been around 150 years old. One thing is certain: he was undeniably proud that he was a gentleman of Virginia — not an Earthman, not American, but a Virginian! (See "John Carter — Past and Present," *ERB-dom* magazine, #24 [Aug., 1968] and #26 [June, 1969].)

The key facts we have concerning this man are found in the Foreword and first chapter of *A Princess of Mars*. We are told he lived and fought for years among the Sioux Indians. He served with the Confederate Army, in which he attained the rank of captain. He spent part of "his strange wild life in all parts of the world." He was a superb horseman, a marvelous swordsman, and a professional fighting man. Physically, Carter was "a good two inches over six feet, broad of shoulder, and narrow of hip, with the carriage of the trained fighting man. His features were regular and clear cut, his hair black and closely cropped, while his eyes were of a steel gray." At the close of the Civil War, he drifted west with a companion, Captain James K. Powell, in search of gold, and in the winter of 1865 they were successful in locating a fabulous mine in Arizona. However, they were attacked by Apaches, Powell was killed, and Carter was forced to hide in a cave. Something spectral or supernatural frightened away the Indians and paralyzed Carter. With a superhuman effort he appeared to break free but to his amazement saw his body lying on the floor before him. Slipping to the mouth of the cave, he held out his arms toward the planet Mars and was almost instantly drawn through space to that distant world.

It was on Mars, or Barsoom, in a moss-covered valley and near a great incubator that John Carter was captured by the Tharks, giant four-armed creatures of that strange land. Here he learned their language, their customs, their problems. He escaped, with another prisoner, Dejah Thoris, Princess of Helium and a human like himself. After many adventures he finally reached the city of Helium, received a hero's welcome, and became the husband of the beautiful Dejah Thoris.

After nearly five happy years (or nine Earth years) in Helium, catastrophe struck. The Atmosphere Plant failed, and the world was dying. Carter managed to open the doors of the plant, and the great motors were turned on but not before he lapsed into unconsciousness. When he recovered, he was back in the cave in Arizona.

Ten lonely years went by before he "died" again, in March, 1886; and moments later he found himself back on Barsoom.

To describe his further adventures herein would be redundant. It is sufficient to say he exposed the evil thern priesthood as spurious prophets; he destroyed the false goddess, Issus; and he opened communication with the nations of the south pole and of the north pole — all in his efforts to rejoin his wife, Dejah Thoris. Because of his great leadership ability, he was given the title Warlord of Mars by the greatest jeddaks of his day.

John Carter eventually discovered how to transport himself across the void between Earth and Barsoom, and thus was able to visit his nephew in America from time to time, and bring him up to date on affairs on the Red Planet. Out there on Barsoom "he still lives" with his incomparable princess, their son, Carthoris, and their daughter, Tara.

Carthoris: {GM/10+; WM/1,8,13,16; TMM/-; CM/Prel.,1; MMM/14; FMM/2; SM/1,10; SMM/1} The son of John Carter and Dejah Thoris. He was born shortly after Carter's successful attempt to reopen the doors of the vital Atmosphere Plant. This would be in 1876, Earth time. The young Prince of Helium inherited much of his father's wild lust for adventure, his skill with the sword, and his superlative physical strength and agility.

While on a rash attempt to explore the south polar region, he was captured by the First Born and held prisoner for a year, before escaping with his father and the black dator, Xodar. Following the defeat of the therns and the Black Pirates, and the death of Zat Arrras, Jed of

Zodanga and Regent of Helium, Carthoris assumed leadership of the empire until the return of his great-grandfather, Tardos Mors.

He fought alongside Tars Tarkas during the invasion of Okar and the eventual rescue of his parents. He fought for and won as his wife the beautiful Thuvia, Princess of Ptarth, whom he first met as a slave girl of the therns.

At one stage of his travels he was known as Turjun the Panthan.

Carthoris had an inquiring mind and was responsible for the pre-set destination control compass and the obstruction evader for aircraft. Other scientists took up the challenge, and the result was a rapid improvement in the design and construction of aircraft in the Heliumatic navy.

Dak Kova: {PM/18,19} Jed of the Warhoons, who captured John Carter after the latter's escape from the Tharks. He challenged and defeated his jeddak, Bar Comas, and thus became leader of the Warhoons.

Dar Tarus: {MMM/6+; SM/2,6} A young warrior attached to the court of Xaxa, Jeddara of Phundahl. He was assassinated and his body exchanged with that of an aging nobleman, Sag Or. He was revived in the body of the nobleman by Vad Varo, and set out with the latter to seek revenge. Eventually he was returned to his own body, Xaxa died, and he became jeddak of Phundahl and High Priest of Tor in her stead.

Dejah Thoris: {PM to JCM(SMJ)} Princess of Helium. Daughter of Mors Kajak, Jed of Lesser Helium, and granddaughter of Tardos Mors, Jeddak of all Helium. "I am the daughter of ten thousand jeddaks... I trace my ancestry straight back without a break to the builder of the first great waterway" (PM/13).

Captured by the Tharks, she was rescued by John Carter, only to fall into the hands of Sab Than, Prince of Zodanga. She was again rescued by Carter, this time with the help of the Tharks, and, shortly after, became the wife of the Virginian. When Carter disappeared (his involuntary return to Earth), she waited and searched in vain, eventually setting out on a pilgrimage to the Valley Dor at about the same time Carter found himself back on the Red Planet. After a long series of adventures ranging from the south pole to the equator to the north pole, the two were reunited and returned to Helium. All this is covered in the first three books.

In the next four books, Dejah Thoris plays very minor roles, but in *SM* she is kidnapped and taken to Thuria, the nearer moon of Barsoom, by a Zodangan scientist and an assassin, only to be rescued again by her husband. Later, she is seriously injured in an air crash and Carter has to enlist the services of Ras Thavas, the Master Mind of Mars, to restore her to her former self. Some years later, both the Warlord and his princess are captured and taken to Jupiter, where the Morgors of that world attempt to secure information toward the conquest of Barsoom. Unfortunately, our chronicles end at this stage and, until further communications are received from Barsoom, we are unable to state just how Dejah Thoris, Princess of Mars, was returned to her beloved Helium.

Djor Kantos: {GM/21; CM/1,2,22} The son of Kantos Kan, overlord of the Heliumatic fleet and close friend of John Carter. Although only a padwar, he was a suitor for the hand of Tara of Helium, daughter of the Warlord. After Tara's disappearance following the great storm that swept across the Twin Cities, he married Oliva Marthis, daughter of the Jed of Hastor.

Dotar Sojat: {PM/14,16; WM/6; SMM/3,6,11; LG-2,3,4} Name given to John Carter by the Tharks. It comes from the surnames of two Thark warriors he killed. He used it on several occasions as an alias, when disguised as a red man.

Doxus: {LG-2/5+} Jeddak of the Black Pirates of Kamtol in the Valley of the First Born. He controlled his subjects through a machine which had recorded each person's individual nerve index and was keyed to impart a paralytic stroke if Doxus so desired.

Dur Ajmad: {SMM/26,27} An Amhorian noble with royal blood and popular with the troops. Doubtless, he succeeded Jal Had as Prince of Amhor, following the latter's death.

Dur-dan: {SMM/15,29} One of Ras Thavas' best hormads. He helped John Carter and the great surgeon escape from Morbus, although he himself was killed in the attempt.

E-Mad: {CM/11-14} A Manatorian. Dwar of the Towers of Jetan. He was killed by Tara of Helium when he attempted to molest her.

Em-Tar: {LG-3/4} A warrior of Kobol, in the forces of Hin Abtol of Panar.

E-Thas: {CM/20+} Sycophantic major-domo in the palace of O-Tar, Jeddak of Manator.

Fal Sivass: {SM/-} A Zodangan scientist and inventor. He designed and built a mentally controlled spacecraft, with a view to visiting Thuria, the nearer moon of Barsoom, which he believed contained vast quantities of gold, platinum, and jewels. Once enriched, he would make even the Warlord of Barsoom kneel to him. His dream failed to materialize because of his own cowardice and sense of insecurity.

Floran: {CM/16-22} A Gatholian enslaved by the Manatorians. He fought as the princess' panthan in the game of Jetan between Gahan of Gathol and U-Dor of Manator. He escaped from Manator, returning with Gatholian and Heliumatic forces to rescue Gahan and Tara of Helium.

Fo-nar: {LG-3/6-10} A "than," or warrior, on the *Dusar*, one of Hin Abtol's ships besieging Gathol. Originally from Jahar, he was now a panthan. John Carter appropriated the ship and made Fo-nar his First Padwar. Later the crew mutinied, but Fo-nar's fate is not disclosed in the chronicles.

Gahan: {CM/-; LG-1/10; LG-3/1,3} Jed of Gathol and husband of Tara of Helium.

He was visiting Helium when Barsoom's worst storm in living memory struck the nation. Tara was swept away in her flier and Gahan set out to rescue her. After a year of adventuring in Bantoom and Manator, the two were rescued. They reside in Gathol and have one daughter, Llana. While in Manator, Gahan used the aliases Turan the panthan and U-Kal of Manataj.

Years later, Gahan was visited by Hin Abtol, Jeddak of Panar, who kidnapped Llana and laid siege to the small mountain country. Hin Abtol was defeated and Llana rescued by John Carter.

Gan Had: {SMM/4-6,16-19,(23),(28)} A Toonolian captive of the hormads of Morbus. He fled into the marshes along with Vor Daj and several other slaves, and was eventually rescued by the Heliumatic fleet.

(NOTE: The book *SMM* shows Pandar the Phundahlian as the one who was rescued, but this is incorrect. Pandar was recaptured by the hormads, along with Sytor and Janai. It was Gan Had who was picked up by the Amhorian ship, along with Tun Gan. So it was actually Gan Had — not Pandar — who leaped overboard and was later rescued by the Ruzaar of Helium; and *he* would have returned to Toonol, not Phundahl.)

Gan-ho: {LG-3/8} An insubordinate crewman on the *Dusar,* the Pandar ship seized by John Carter. Rather than face the Warlord, he leaped overboard.

Gan Hor: {LG-3/2-4} A dwar in one of the utans of warrior-herdsmen of Gathol during the siege of Hin Abtol.

Gantun Got: {SMM/8,9,23,25; LG-2/5} Head of the Assassins' Guild of Amhor. Captured by the hormads of Morbus, his brain was destroyed and his body given to the hormad Tor-dur-bar, who then changed his name to Tun-gan or Tun Gan. Ironically enough, Tun-gan is taken to Amhor, where he assumes the identity of Gantun Gur.

Gar Nal: {SM/3+} A Zodangan inventor and tool of the Assassins' Guild of Zodanga. His spacecraft reached Thuria before that of Fal Sivas, which was piloted by John Carter. Eventually the two inventors combined forces, but they were bested by the Warlord.

Ghek: {CM/5+} A kaldane from the swarm of Luud in the nation of Bantoom. Captivated by the singing of Tara of Helium, he helped her and Gahan of Gathol escape from the burrows of Luud, and further aided them while prisoners in Manator. He and his rikor now live in Helium.

Ghron: {FMM/8,9} The mad jed of Ghasta, in the Valley Hohr. His chief form of pleasure was the torturing and maiming of his slaves.

Gor-don: {LG-3/10-12} A padwar rescued by John Carter from a disabled Panar ship. Later, the Warlord's crew mutinied and put the two of them on the ground. They then walked to Pankor, Gor-don's home.

Gorgum: {JCM(SMJ)/7} An officer in the guard of the emperor of the Morgors.

Gor Hajus: {MMM/6+} A famous and popular Toonolian assassin. Executed on orders from the jeddak of Toonol, his body was sold to

Ras Thavas, the Master Mind of Barsoom. Revived by Vad Varo (Ulysses Paxton), he became a loyal ally and friend, and eventually became the voice of Tur, under Dar Tarus, Jeddak of Phundahl.

Gozava: {PM/15,24} A green woman, the secret mate of Tars Tarkas, a warrior of Thark. She was the mother of Sola. She was tortured to death by Tal Hajus, Jeddak of Thark.

Gridley, Jason: {FMM/F'word} A young American and a neighbor of Edgar Rice Burroughs in Tarzana, California. He discovered a new type of radio wave with which he was able to communicate with Pellucidar (see *Tanar of Pellucidar*) and, later, with Barsoom.

Gur Tus: {GM/21} Dwar of the 10th Utan of the Heliumatic troops, which invaded Omean and helped capture the Temple of Issus.

Had Urtur: {FMM/1} Odwar of the 1st Umak of the troops of Hastor. His wife is a princess of Gathol, and his son is Tan Hadron of Hastor. *See also Tan Hadron.*

Haglion: {JCM(SMJ)/3} Commander of the Morgor spaceship that brought the kidnapped John Carter from Barsoom to Jupiter.

Haja: {CM/14} A princess of Gathol, and aunt of its jed, Gahan. Captured and enslaved by Manatorians, she bore a son, A-Kor, to O-Tar, the jeddak, who then gave her to U-Thor, Jed of Manatos. U-Thor made her a free woman and married her.

Haj Alt: {FMM/11} The son of Haj Osis, and thus Prince of Tjanath.

Haj Osis: {FMM/5-7,11,12} Jed of Tjanath, a small nation that lived in fear of attack from the ships of Jahar.

Hal Vas: {TMM/11-13} Dwar of the Southern Road, a portion of one of Dusar's canals. The son of Vas Kor, a nobleman of Dusar.

Hamas: {SM/3-13} Major-domo of the house of Fal Sivas in Zodanga. A pompous but cowardly individual.

Han Do: {JCM(SMJ)/7+} A Savator, or blue-skinned Jovian. A prisoner of the Morgors, he escaped, along with John Carter and several other slaves.

Hin Abtol: {LG/-} A red man and self-termed Jeddak of Jeddaks of the North. Actually he was Jeddak of Panar, a section of arctic land apart from Okar but having a hothouse city similar to those in Okar. Panarians are few in number and a backward race, so Hin Abtol conceived the idea of taking prisoners and then placing them in cold storage until he had sufficient troops to conquer all Barsoom. He kidnapped Llana of Gathol, granddaughter of John Carter, and laid siege to Gathol; but he was ultimately captured by the Warlord.

Ho Ran Kim: {LG-1/3-7} Jeddak of Horz, and leader of a small band of Orovars, descendants of the ancient white-skinned rulers of Barsoom.

Hora San: {MMM/11,14} Former jeddak and High Priest of Phundahl, whose strange disappearance a century ago was never explained until Vad Varo and Gor Hajus discovered his bones within the great image of the god Tur.

Hor Kai Lan:{LG-1/8,9} Brother of the jeddak of Horz when it was a thriving metropolis over a million years ago. He was placed in a state of suspended animation by Lum Tar O and revived only when John Carter beheaded the latter. Shortly afterward Hor Kai Lan disintegrated into dust.

Hortan Gur: {TMM/5,11} Notorious jeddak of the green men of Torquas.

Horur: {JCM(SMJ)/7} A Morgor of Sasoom, or Jupiter. He was a high-ranking officer in the court of his emperor, Bandolian.

Hor Vastus: {GM/16-18,22} An officer in the navy of Helium, and the first to greet John Carter after the latter's escape from the Valley Dor. Later, he was instrumental in building up a naval force to attempt to rescue Dejah Thoris from the First Born.

Hovan Du: {MMM/3,7+} A native of Ptarth, his body was obtained by Ras Thavas, the Master Mind of Mars, who removed half his brain and placed it in the skull of a white ape. The ape was revived by Vad Varo and became a strong ally in the latter's attempt to rescue Valla Dia. Later, his brain was reunited in his human skull and he became a priest of Tur, in Phundahl.

I-Gos: {CM/15+} Taxidermist extraordinary. An old man of Manator, bent and wrinkled with age—a rare sight On Barsoom. He was responsible for disclosing O-Tar, Jeddak of Manator, as a coward.

Il-dur-en:{SMM/15} One of Ras Thavas' most intelligent and loyal hormads.

I-Mal: {CM/16,18} A dead chief of Manator, from whose embalmed body Gahan of Gathol appropriated harness and arms.

Issus: {GM/9+} Ruler of the First Born, the black-skinned race of Barsoom, and hailed as the Goddess of Death and of Eternal Life for all Barsoomians. She was also addressed as Daughter of the Lesser Moon. In truth, she was a wrinkled old hag—toothless, bald, and cannibalistic. She went mad when she was thwarted and exposed by John Carter, and was torn to pieces by her own followers.

I-Zav: {CM/12,14} A guard in the cells of Manator. He was hypnotized and disarmed by his prisoner, Ghek the kaldane.

Jad-han: {LG-2/5,6,13; LG-3/1,13; LG-4/13} A citizen of Amhor, and a brother of Janai. He was captured and enslaved by the First Born of Kamtol, but escaped with John Carter. He was taken prisoner by the Panars and held until freed following the lifting of the siege of Gathol.

Jal Had: {MMM/4; SMM/16,23-27} Prince, or jed, of Amhor. An enormous individual, he tried in vain to abduct Valla Dia, daughter of the jeddak of Duhor. Some time later he sought Janai of Amhor as one of his wives. His other hobby was collecting specimens for his zoo. He was killed by a green Martian, one of his own exhibits.

Janai: {SMM/-; LG-2/5} A girl of Amhor, she fled because Jal Had, Prince of Amhor, wanted her as one of his wives. She was captured by the hormads of Morbus but escaped with the help of Vor Daj of Helium, whom she later wed. She has a brother, Jad-han.

Jat Or: {SM/10+} A young padwar in the personal guard of Dejah Thoris, Princess of Helium. He accompanied John Carter to Thuria in an effort to rescue their princess from a band of assassins. While on this mission, he met and fell in love with Zanda of Zodanga.

Jav: {TMM/6-10} A Lotharian. He ranked second to Tario, Jeddak of Lothar, in this new Lothar in the Mountains of Torquas. He and his compatriots would be at least half a million years old, if his story is true. He was killed by the banth, Komal.

Kab Kadja: {GM/14} Jed of the Warhoons of the South, one of the green tribes of Barsoom.

Kal Tavan: {FMM/1,2,16} A slave in the employ of Tor Hatan of Hastor. He saw and identified the abductors of Sanoma Tora, his master's daughter. He was later freed and made a dwar by John Carter. Following this, he revealed that he was the son of a former jed of Tjanath, and the father of the girl Tavia.

Kam Han Tor: {LG-1/9-12} A renowned shipbuilder of ancient Horz and brother of the jeddak of his day.

Placed in a state of suspended animation by Lum Tar O, he recovered a million years later, only to crumble into dust within an hour or so.

Kandus: {LG-4/2-9} One of the men of Invak who captured John Carter and Llana of Gathol in the Forest of Lost Men.

Kantos Kan: {PM/19-26; GM/16+; WM/14,16; CM/1} A padwar, or lieutenant, in the navy of Helium, he was captured by the green Warhoons while searching their city for some trace of his missing princess, Dejah Thoris. John Carter was cast into the same cell and the two men became fast friends. Following their escape, they subsequently met in Zodanga, where Dejah Thoris was known to be a prisoner. With the assistance of the Tharks, now led by Tars Tarkas, Zodanga was taken and Dejah Thoris, John Carter, and Kantos Kan returned to Helium in triumph.

Eventually Kantos Kan became overlord of the navy of Helium, and fought with John Carter in defeating the therns and the First Born in the Otz Mountains and the Valley Dor. Later, he led the navy into Okar to rescue his beloved princess and her family.

Kara Vasa: {MMM/12,14} The sweetheart of Dar Tarus of Phundahl. She fled to Helium, but returned to marry him after he became jeddak of Phundahl.

Kar Komak: {TMM/10+; CM/Prel.} A bowman materialized by Tario of Lothar, and the first to retain his existence.

In his former existence, over half a million years ago, he was commander of the fleets of Lothar, and known and respected throughout Barsoom.

Komal: *see Part IV, "The Flora and Fauna of Barsoom."*

Kor-an: {LG-3/2-4} A warrior-herdsman of Gathol, he captured John Carter following the latter's escape from Kamtol.

Kor San: {MMM/4,14} Jeddak of Duhor and father of Valla Dia.

Kulan Tith: {WM/5-7,16; TMM/1,13,14} Jeddak of Kaol, that small, forested nation astride the equator and adjoining its ally, Parth.

Espoused to Thuvia of Ptarth, he withdrew his claim when he learned she loved Carthoris of Helium.

Lakor: {WM/2,3} A thern in the retinue of Matai Shang, Father of Therns. He was killed by Woola, deep within the Otz Mountains.

Lan-O: {CM/11-13,17,18} A Gatholian girl enslaved by the Manatorians. She served as the Orange Princess in the game of Jetan involving Tara of Helium.

Lan Sohn Wen: {LG-1/3-5} Dwar of the 1st Utan of the Jeddak's Guard, which captured John Carter when he landed in Horz.

Larok: {TMM/2} A warrior-artificer in the service of Vas Hor, a nobleman of Dusar.

Lee Um Lo: {LG-1/5,9} An Orovar embalmer of a million years ago. His work in the pits of Horz was so perfect that not even the corpse himself knew he was dead.

Llana of Gathol: {LG/-} Daughter of Tara of Helium and Gahan of Gathol. Granddaughter of Dejah Thoris and John Carter. Kidnapped by Hin Abtol, Jeddak of Panar, she escaped but met with a series of adventures along with John Carter and an Orovar, Pan Dan Chee, of Horz, before returning safely to Gathol.

Lorquas Ptomel: {PM/7-16,24} A green Barsoomian. Jed of the band of Tharks that captured John Carter after his initial arrival on the Red Planet.

Lum Tar O: {LG-1/8,9} A resident of ancient Horz, whose only friend was Lee Um Lo, Barsoom's greatest embalmer, who did such a fine job on Lum Tar O when he died that his body kept on functioning. Over the centuries, Lum Tar O placed many of the citizens of Horz in a state of suspended animation that lasted until his decapitation by John Carter a million years later.

Luud: {CM/4-8,14} Bi-sexual king of a swarm of kaldanes in Bantoom. He was slain by one of his own subjects, Ghek, who then escaped with Tara of Helium and Gahan of Gathol.

Man-lat: {LG-2/10,12} A junior officer in the palace of Doxus, Jeddak of Kamtol. He was detailed to guard the slave, Dotar Sojat.

Matai Shang: {GM/5+; WM/-} The Father of Therns. Leader of the white-skinned race of Barsoom, who serve as priests of Issus, the goddess of most Barsoomians. The falseness of his religion exposed, he fled from the Mountain of Otz and was eventually killed in Okar by the black dator, Thurid.

Moak: {CM/4} King of one of the swarms of kaldanes of Bantoom.

Mors Kajak: {PM/10,21,26,27; GM/16-19; WM/1,9-16} Jed of Lesser Helium. The son of Tardos Mors, and the father of Dejah Thoris. An outstanding warrior with a reputation for ferocity and fearlessness.

Motus: {LG-4/3-11} A nobleman of Invak. He kicked the shackled John Carter, who later killed him in a duel before the jeddak of Invak.

Multis Par: {JCM(SMJ)/1-7} The son of Zu Tith, the tyrannical Jed of Zor who was killed when the city was conquered by Helium. Captured by the Morgors of Sasoom, or Jupiter, he was used as a pawn in their efforts to invade and conquer Barsoom.

Mu Tel: {MMM/8,9} Prince of the House of Kan, in the city of Toonol. A nephew of the jeddak, and a friend of Gor Hajus the assassin. He helped Vad Varo and his companions escape from Toonol.

Myr-lo: {LG-2/5+} A scientist of the First Born of Kamtol. He was responsible for the mechanism in which was recorded the "nerve index" of every person in Kamtol—except the jeddak—and who thus were at its mercy. He was killed by John Carter.

Nastor: {LG-2/7+} A dator, or prince, of the First Born of Kamtol. He purchased the enslaved Llana of Gathol, but was killed by John Carter in a successful rescue attempt.

Nolat: {LG-2/8-12} A dator, or prince, of Kamtol, who was beaten in a duel with John Carter.

Notan: {PM/22} The royal psychologist to Than Kosis, Jeddak of Zodanga. He could read the last-minute impressions on the mind of a slain man.

Nur An: {FMM/5+} Member of a Jaharan family of ancient lineage and great wealth. His property was confiscated by Tul Axtar, Jeddak of Jahar, and he was forced to flee for his life. Imprisoned by the jeddak of Tjanath, he was sentenced to "The Death," along with Hadron of Hastor. After many strange adventures, the two succeeded in reaching the safety of Helium and the arms of their loved ones.

Nutus: {TMM/12+} Jeddak of Dusar and father of Prince Astok, the abductor of Thuvia of Ptarth.

O Ala: {JCM(SMJ)/9} The wife of Han Du, the Savator with whom John Carter escaped from the Morgors.

Olvia Marthis: {CM/1,2,22} Daughter of the Jed of Hastor. She married Djor Kantos, son of Kantos Kan.

O-Mai the Cruel: {CM/18+} Jeddak of Manator some five thousand years ago. He died with an expression of fear so great that it drove to madness those who looked at him. Thus, his bones still lie in the now-shunned apartment where he died.

Orm-O: {SMM/24-27} A young Duhorian boy, slave in the palace of the jeddak of Amhor. He was detailed to feed Tor-dur-bar, the "Hormad from Morbus," who was encaged in the Amhorian Zoo.

O-Tar: {CM/10+} Jeddak of Manator. A ruthless, self-centered man who still believed in Corphals—spirits of the evil dead. Accused of cowardice, he took his own life.

O-Zar: {CM/16} A swordsman from Manataj, famed for his skill on the Fields of Jetan.

Ozara: {SM/18+} The enforced jeddara of the Tarids of Ladan, or Thuria. She was abducted from her homeland, Domnia, by agents of Ul Vas, Jeddak of the Tarids. With the aid of John Carter she escaped, and returned safely to Domnia.

Pan Dan Chee: {LG/-} A resident of Horz and direct descendant of the pre-drought race of Orovars.

Fleeing Horz with John Carter and Llana of Gathol, he fought a banth, Black Pirates, and Panarians in an effort to win the beautiful Llana.

Pandar: {SMM/4-6,16-20,(23),(28)} A Phundahlian prisoner of the hormads of Morbus. He escaped with Vor Daj, Janai, Gan Had, Sytor, and Tun Gan. He and Sytor abducted Janai, but the three of them were soon recaptured by the hormads. The ultimate fate of Pandar and Sytor is not disclosed.

(NOTE: In Chap. 23 of *SMM* we read that Pandar and Tur Gan deserted Vor Daj and were later captured by Amhorians. This is incorrect, and "Pandar" should read "Gan Had." Also, he would try to reach Toonol rather than Phundahl. This error continues in Chap. 28, where we read that a ship from Helium picked up Pandar. This, too, should read "Gan Had.")

Parthak: {GM/19} A young Zodangan in the service of Zat Arrras in his palace in Helium. He was warder for the imprisoned John Carter.

Paxton, Ulysses: {MMM/-; FMM/f'word; SMM/1,2,6,9} Late Captain,—th Inf., U.S. Army in World War I. Hit by a German shell in France, he broke away from his earthly body and moments later found himself in a castle yard on what he soon learned was Barsoom, that world to which John Carter, had preceded him a half-century earlier.

His captor and host was the famous Ras Thavas, the Master Mind of Mars. Here Paxton, now renamed Vad Varo, learned the language and customs of his new home. Ras Thavas trained him in the field of surgery until the American could graft limbs from one body to another, perform internal organ transplants, and even transfer a brain from one cranium to another. Thus, he was able to remove Ras Thavas' brain from his aging body and place it in the body of a much younger red man.

In the meantime Paxton, or Vad Varo, had fallen in love with Valla Dia, a beautiful Duhorian whose body Ras Thavas had purchased and then sold to the disfigured Xaxa, Jeddara of Phundahl. The brains of the two women were switched and it became Vad Varo's avowed intention to return his sweetheart's brain to its proper body. This he did, after a series of adventures—and with the help of companions rescued from the vaults of Ras Thavas. He married Valla Dia, who turned out to be the daughter of the jeddak of Duhor. They spent their honeymoon in Helium, upon the invitation of John Carter, Warlord of Barsoom.

Phaidor: {GM/7-11,22; WM/-} Daughter of Matai Shang, spiritual and imperial leader of the white-skinned therns.

Captured by the First Born, she was imprisoned with Dejah Thoris and Thuvia of Ptarth in the Temple of the Sun. Freed by her father and the black dator, Thurid, they fled to Okar, where eventually she killed Thurid and then committed suicide.

Phao: {FMM/6-7,11-17} A Jaharian girl, sweetheart of Nur An. She was sold into slavery in Tjanath. Rescued by Hadron of Hastor, she eventually rejoined her lover.

Pho Lar: {JCM(SMJ)/7+} A blue-skinned Savator of Jupiter. One of a group imprisoned, along with John Carter, by the Morgors. Under the leadership of the Warlord, they escaped to safety in the jungle. Pho Lar eventually reached his own country.

Phor San: {LG-3/5-9} An odwar in the fleet of Panar, which was besieging Gathol. While drunk, he appointed John Carter a dwar of one of his ships. Later, while attempting to reverse his decision, he was taken prisoner and thrown overboard.

Phor Tak: {FMM/5,9+} A scientist of Jahar, and the inventor of a rifle which projected rays that caused metals to disintegrate. Falling into disfavor with Tul Axtar, his jeddak, he swore revenge; and in a private laboratory at Jhama he created the "Flying Death," an un-manned craft that would track down and destroy any ship at which it was directed. Another invention was paint which rendered objects invisible. His plans for vengeance, and to conquer all Barsoom, were foiled by his own cowardice. He was killed by Hadron of Hastor.

Phystal: {SM/3,11,13} A Zodangan in charge of the slaves of Fal Sivas, the inventor.

Pnoxus: {LG-4/2-6,9} Prince of Invak. Son of the jeddak, Ptantus. He captured John Carter and Llana of Gathol when they landed in the Forest of Lost Men. An obnoxious fellow.

Povak: {SM/8,9} A Zodangan. A member of Ur Jan's band of as-sassins. His efforts to murder the panthan Vandor, who was actually John Carter, resulted in his own death.

Powell, James K.: {PM/1} An ex-Confederate Army Captain. A prospecting companion of John Carter, and co-discoverer of a gold mine in Arizona in 1865. He was killed by Apaches while attempting to obtain supplies.

Ptang: {LG-2/6-9} A warrior in the retinue of Xaxak, a dator of Kamtol, in the Valley of the First Born.

Defeated in a duel with John Carter, who was going by the name of Dotar Sojat, he then became a good friend of the Warlord.

Ptantus: {LG-4/2-12} Jeddak of Invak, in the Forest of Lost Men. A loudmouthed, conceited man.

Ptor Fak: {PM/20; LG-4/4+} A Zodangan government official and overseer of the farmland along one of the nation's canals. One of three brothers who befriended John Carter early in his existence on Barsoom. Years later, he again encountered the Virginian, when both were prisoners in the city of Invak.

Rab-zov: {LG-3/13} A member of Hin Abtol's bodyguard, and reputed to be the strongest man in Pankor.
He was bested by John Carter in a wrestling match.

Rapas: {SM/-} A petty Zodangan assassin, he worked for both Fal Sivas, the inventor, and Ur Jan, head of the Assassins' Guild of Zodanga. Because of his double-dealings he was known as Rapas the Ulsio (or Rat).

Ras Thavas: {MMM/-; SMM/-} The Master Mind of Mars. Barsoom's greatest surgeon, and a Toonolian nobleman. At first, an old man, wrinkled and withered, with a large cranium, and wearing large multi-lensed glasses and a hearing aid. He lived on his family estate, parts of which were built twenty-three thousand years ago; and here he maintained his laboratory. It lay on the edge of the Great Toonolian Marshes, not too far from the city of Toonol.
Ras Thavas knew the human anatomy so well he could transfer any part of one body to any other body. Limbs, internal organs, and even brains could be replaced under his skilled direction. Weird experiments were tried, such as a woman's brain in a man's body, or half an animal's brain with half a man's brain. He taught his skill to Vad Varo, who had been Ulysses Paxton of the U.S.A., and then had Vad Varo transfer his (Ras Thavas') brain to the body of a splendid young red man.

Eventually driven from his castle by Vobis Kan, Jeddak of Toonol, he set up his headquarters at Morbus, a deserted city built in prehistoric times on an island along the edge of the marshes. Here he attempted to create synthetic human life. He was too successful: the "hormads" rebelled and imprisoned him. He escaped with the aid of John Carter, who then had Morbus and its life-form completely destroyed. It is assumed Ras Thavas now practices in Helium.

Rojas: {LG-4/3+} A beautiful Invak girl, she helped John Carter to escape from the Forest of Lost Men and beguiled him into taking her to Helium with him.

Ro Tan Bim: {LG-I/8} A resident of ancient Horz placed in a state of suspended animation by the mad Lum Tar O a million or so years ago.

Sab Than: {PM/21-25} Prince or jed of Zodanga. Son of Than Kosis, Jeddak of Zodanga. At war with Helium, he agreed to stop hostilities if Dejah Thoris, Princess of Helium, would marry him. He was killed by Tharks in a battle which interrupted the wedding ceremony.

Sag Or: {MMM/11+} A Phundahlian nobleman of unprepossessing appearance. He had a young guardsman of Xaxa's court, Dar Tarus, assassinated and then had Ras Thavas, the great surgeon, transfer his brain to the body of the younger man. He was subsequently returned to his own body, although not by his own choosing.

Salensus Oll: {WM/9+} Jeddak of Jeddaks of Okar, land of the yellow-skinned race of Barsoom. "A cruel and tyrannous master whom all hate" (WM/9). So said his nephew, Talu. He held Tardos Mors, Jeddak of Helium; Mors Kajak, Jed of Lesser Helium; and many of their troops prisoner in Okar, where they had crashed in a vain search for Carthoris.

John Carter entered Okar on the trail of the abducted Dejah Thoris, only to find that Salensus Oll planned to marry her. In the ensuing struggle, the jeddak was killed by Carter and the throne turned over to his nephew, Talu, Prince of Marentina.

Sanoma Tora: {FMM/-} The beautiful but vain daughter of Tor Hatan, Odwar of the 91st Umak of the troops of Helium, and a man of great wealth. She rebuffed her suitor, Tan Hadron of Hastor, in favor of Tul Axtar, Jeddak of Jahar, but in the end lost both.

San Tothis: {CM/3,7} Commander of the cruiser *Vanator*, used by Gahan of Gathol on his visit to Helium.
He and his crew were swept away to an unknown fate in the most violent storm ever to strike modern-day Barsoom.

Saran Tal: {TMM/2,3} Major-domo in the palace of Carthoris of Helium. He purchased Vas Kor, a Dusarian noble, who was masquerading as a slave.

Sarkoja: {PM/9-24} A Thark woman. One of the senior members of the retinue of Tars Tarkas. A cruel and ruthless person, she bore a deep hatred for the gentle Sola and had earlier been responsible for the horrible death of Sola's mother. She was eventually banished from the tribe.

Sator Throg: {GM/4,5} A Holy Thern of the Tenth Cycle and a former master of the red slave girl, Thuvia, who shot him while attempting to escape from the Otz Mountains with John Carter. Physically, except for their hair, he was a double for the Virginian.

Sept: {CM/5} A kaldane of the swarm of Luud, and high in the latter's retinue.

Sharu: {FMM/8,9} A beautiful member of the court of Ghron, the mad jed of Ghasta. She helped Hadron of Hastor as well as Nur An to escape from the Valley Hohr.

Sil Vagis: {FMM/1} A teedwar on the staff of Tor Hatan of Helium, and suitor for the hand of his daughter, Sanoma Tora. He was with her when she was kidnapped, but fled in panic when the abductors approached.

Sola: {PM/4-27; GM/16-18} A green woman of the Thark tribe. John Carter's teacher and guide when he first landed on Barsoom. Sola differed from the cruel, loveless members of her kind inasmuch as she knew who her parents were, and she felt both compassion and affection for others. She was the daughter of Tars Tarkas and Gozava, and a true friend of John Carter and Dejah Thoris.

Solan: {WM/12+} A yellow-skinned Okarian in charge of the switch-room beneath the jeddak's palace in Kadabra. He was "a little, wizened-up, pasty-faced old fellow" *(WM/12)*, but still one of the best swordsmen John Carter ever encountered. He died beneath the Earthman's blade while defending the switch that controlled the great magnetic tower, the Guardian of the North.

Soran: *see Sovan.*

Sorav: {WM/10} An Okarian. Commander of the troops in the palace of Salensus Oll, Jeddak of Jeddaks of Okar.

Sovan: {WM/7,8; TMM/1; CM/1} Prince of Ptarth. The son of Thuvan Dihn, Jeddak of Ptarth, and the brother of Thuvia. He commanded the fleets of Ptarth and ruled the nation when his father was visiting Kaol and in Okar.
   (NOTE: In CM, he appears as Prince Soran of Ptarth.)

Sytor: {SMM/4,13-20,29} Dwar in charge of the party of hormads that captured John Carter and Vor Daj near the Toonolian Marshes. It is believed he was a normal red man, from Dusar. He abducted Janai while escaping from Morbus, but both were recaptured. His fate is unknown.

Tal Hajus: {PM/9-17,24} Cruel, cunning, and degenerate jeddak of the green tribe of Tharks that captured John Carter when the latter first found himself on Barsoom. He threatened to ravish Dejah Thoris but was knocked out by Carter, and the two escaped. He was killed later by Tars Tarkas in a duel for leadership of the Tharks.

Talu: {WM/9+; TMM/13; CM/1; LG-1/10} Prince of Marentina, a principality in the nation of Okar, land of the yellow men. At odds with his uncle, Salensus Oll, Jeddak of Okar, he aided John Carter in his efforts to rescue Dejah Thoris, and subsequently, upon the death of his uncle, became jeddak of the arctic nation.

Tan Gama: {GM/14,15} A member of the green Warhoons of the South. One of those detailed to guard the captured Tars Tarkas. He was killed by John Carter.

Tan Hadron: {FMM/-; LG-3/7-10} A padwar in the troops of Helium and the son of Had Urtur, a naval commander of Hastor. His mother is a princess of Gathol. When Sanoma Tora, the girl he was courting, was abducted by the jeddak of Jahar, Tan Hadron set out to rescue her. He was pursued by white apes in Xanator, sentenced to death in Tjanath, imprisoned in Ghasta, and forced to cooperate with the mad inventor, Phor Tak, before eventually succeeding in his mission. He realizes he does not love Sanoma Tora; instead, his true princess is the little slave girl, Tavia, whom he had rescued from a tribe of green men.

Years later, while searching for Llana of Gathol, he is captured by troops of Hin Abtol, Jeddak of Panar. He escapes with John Carter but is recaptured, and to this day his fate is not known.

Tanus: {CM/3} A crewman on the *Vanator,* Gahan of Gathol's ship which set out in the great storm to seek Tara of Helium.

Tara of Helium: {CM/-; MMM/14; FMM/1; LG/F'word; LG-1/6} The daughter of John Carter and Dejah Thoris. She inherited the beauty of her mother and the determination of her father. Swept away in a storm while out in her one-man flier, she was captured by the kaldanes of Bantoom but escaped with the help of Ghek, a kaldane, and Gahan, Jed of Gathol—who was posing as Turan the panthan. Captured again, this time by Manatorians, she is made queen of a live game of Jetan. Later, O-Tar, Jeddak of Manator, tries to force her to marry him, but she is rescued by Gahan and a force of invading Gatholian and Heliumatic troops.

She is now the wife of Gahan of Gathol and the mother of Llana of Gathol.

Tardos Mors: {PM/13+; GM/F'word,3,4,16-19; WM/1,9-16} Jeddak of the empire of Helium, father of Mors Kajak, and grandfather of Dejah Thoris. "He was an almost perfect specimen of manhood; tall, straight as an arrow, superbly muscled and with the carriage and bearing of a ruler of men" (*PM/26*).

Tario: {TMM/6-10} A white-skinned Orovar and the jeddak of Lothar, a city in a crater or valley deep in the Mountains of Torquas. Formerly jeddak of the ancient seaport of Lothar, half a world away, on the shores of the Throxeus Ocean half a million years ago, he led his people over dying sea bottoms to this new haven, as they fled from pursuing green savages. He is an etherealist, believing that "there is no such thing as matter — that all is mind" (*TMM/7*). To him no one exists, except in the imagination of others, other than as an intangible mentality. He has the ability to create men, send them out to fight his enemies, and then dematerialize them when their mission is accomplished.

Tars Tarkas: {PM/-; GM/-; WM/1,8,13,16} A giant green warrior who rose from simple herdsman to jeddak of the Tharks, mightiest of the green hordes of Barsoom. He was the first Barsoomian encountered by John Carter and the two became staunch, lifelong friends.

Differing from his loveless fellow-tribesmen, Tars Tarkas had wooed a green female, Gozava, who bore him a daughter, Sola, before Gozava was tortured to death by her jeddak, Tal Hajus. Later, he slew his chieftain, acknowledged he was the father of Sola, and brought his tribe into an alliance with the empire of Helium. He fought shoulder to shoulder with John Carter against the Warhoons, the plant men, the therns, the First Born; and led his troops in the conquest of Zodanga, as well as of Kadabra in the frozen north.

Tasor: {CM/ 18+} A nobleman of Gathol who was captured by soldiers from Manataj. He was sold to a princess of that city, whom he later married. They moved to Manator, taking new names and starting life anew, he becoming A-Sor the Manatorian. Recognizing Turan the panthan as his former jed, he assisted him and Tara of Helium in their efforts to escape from Manator.

Tavia: {FMM/-; LG-3/7} A slave girl who had escaped from the harem of Tul Axtar, Jeddak of Jahar. She was captured by green men near Xanator, but rescued by Tan Hadron, who was seeking the kidnapped Sanoma Tora. Tavia accompanied him on his search, and ultimately became his wife. It was later revealed that she was the daughter of Kal Tavan, dwar in the navy of Helium and former prince of Tjanath.

Teeaytan-ov: {SMM/4,9-18} One of the hormads in the party that captured John Carter and Vor Daj near the Great Toonolian Marshes. His name means "eleven-hundred-seven." He was killed while attempting to leave Morbus with Vor Daj.

Thabis: {GM/11} A giant First Born whose responsibility was to select the female slave who will then become a meal for Issus, Goddess of Eternal Life.

Than Kosis: {PM/21-25} Jeddak of Zodanga, and the father of Sab Than. He laid siege to the Twin Cities of Helium and demanded that Dejah Thoris marry his son. He was killed by John Carter while taking part in the wedding service.

Thar Ban: {TMM/4,5,11} A jed of one of the green tribes of Torquas. He stole Thuvia of Ptarth from her Dusarian abductors at Aaanthor and fled with her into the Mountains of Torquas. She was rescued by the pursuing Carthoris of Helium.

Thurid: {GM/10; WM/-} A dator, or prince, of the First Born of the Valley Dor. Humiliated by John Carter, who bound him in his own harness in the garden of Issus, he sought revenge through the imprisoned Dejah Thoris. He combined forces with Matai Shang, the Father of Therns, in an effort to gain vengeance upon the Virginian. Together they freed Dejah Thoris and fled across Barsoom, to Kaol, and on to Okar in the frozen north. Here a quarrel developed: Thurid killed Matai Shang, but was himself slain by Phaidor, daughter of the thern chief.

Thuvan Dihn: {WM/7+; TMM/1-3,10-13} Jeddak of Ptarth, the second-most-powerful nation on Barsoom. He is the father of Thuvia and Sovan. While visiting his ally Kulan Tith, Jeddak of Kaol, he met John Carter and the two of them set out for the arctic regions in search of Dejah Thoris and Thuvia. After a series of adventures in the Carrion Caves and Okar, each was united with his loved one. Some time later, through Dusarian duplicity, Ptarth and Kaol were drawn into a war against Helium; however, confrontation was averted at the last moment, and Thuvia of Ptarth became the bride of Carthoris, Prince of Helium.

Thuvia: {GM/-; WM/-; TMM/-} Maid of Mars, a slave of the therns, Princess of Ptarth, wife of Carthoris of Helium. For some unexplained reason, fifteen years before John Carter's advent on Barsoom, this daughter of Thuvan Dihn took the voluntary pilgrimage down the River Iss. Here she was enslaved by the therns in their Otz fortress, until rescued by Carter and Tars Tarkas. Captured by the Black Pirates, she was imprisoned in the Temple of the Sun, along with Dejah Thoris and Phaidor, daughter of Matai Shang. Released by Thurid, the black dator, she was taken to Okar but was eventually rescued by troops from Ptarth and Helium.

Back in her father's palace, she was courted by Carthoris of Helium and by Astok, Prince of Dusar, although she was betrothed to Kulan Tith, Jeddak of Kaol. Abducted by the Dusarian, who cast the blame on Carthoris, she was taken to the deserted city of Aaanthor, near the Mountains of Torquas. Captured by a green man, she was rescued by the Prince of Helium. The pair then encountered Tario the etherealist, Jeddak of Lothar, but fled with his creation, Kar Komak the bowman.

After further adventures, the three rescued Kulan Tith from a band of Torquasians. He freed Thuvia from her bond and she married Carthoris.

Tor-dur-bar: {SMM/-} One of the hormads of Morbus. The name means "four-million-eight." Beheaded by John Carter, he grew a new body but chose to have his brain transferred to the body of an assassin, Gantun Gur, of Amhor. He was renamed Tun-gan, or Tun Gan. He then escaped from Morbus and reached Amhor, where he was accepted as Gantun Gur.

In the meantime, Vor Daj of Helium had his brain transferred to the body of Tor-dur-bar, in an effort to conceal his own identity and better his chances of rescuing Janai of Amhor from the hormads. Thus, *he* was Tor-dur-bar until restored to his own body by Ras Thavas.

Tor Hatan: {FMM/1,2} A lesser noble of Helium. He held the position of odwar of the 91st Umak of the troops of Helium. He was an extremely wealthy man and the father of the beautiful Sanoma Tora.

Torith: {GM/12} A prince, or dator, of the First Born. He was in charge of the guard at the submarine pool at the time of the uprising of the slaves, led by John Carter and Carthoris.

Torkar Bar: {WM/5} Dwar of the Kaolian Road, whose duty it was to patrol the highways that ran throughout the forest. He saved John Carter from being killed by a sith.

Tul Axtar: {FMM/-} Jeddak of Jahar, a city-state lying to the northwest of the Mountains of Torquas.

A vain and arrogant man, whose hobby was collecting beautiful women for his harem—he had several thousand thus enslaved—and whose aim was to conquer all Barsoom. For this purpose he took steps to build up his manpower, until soon his country was badly over-populated. He had his scientists develop weapons capable of disinte-grating metals; with these, he armed his fleet in preparation for an assault on the rest of the world. He struck at the fleet of Helium and success seemed imminent, until Tan Hadron of Hastor thwarted the attack in a ship armed with Tul Axtar's own weapons. The jeddak was killed, Jahar was conquered, and peace restored.

Tun-gan or Tun Gan: {SMM/9-23} Name taken by the hormad Tor-dur-bar after he was given the body of Gantun Gur, former assas-sin of Amhor.

Turan: {CM/8+} Alias used by Gahan of Gathol when posing as a panthan rather than reveal his identity to Tara of Helium.

Turjun: {TMM/13} Alias assumed by Carthoris of Helium, to hide his identity from the Dusarians while he sought the whereabouts of Thuvia of Ptarth.

U Dan: {JCM(SMJ)/2-7} Formerly a padwar in the jeddak's guard at Zor, and a companion of Multis Par, Prince of Zor. He was pledged to marry Vaja, a cousin of the prince. When Vaja was kidnapped and taken to Sasoom, or Jupiter, U Dan was forced to help the Morgors of that world to abduct John Carter. Later, Dejah Thoris also fell into the hands of the Skeleton Men; but she and U Dan escaped, although the Virginian was recaptured. So far, a check of the Carter papers has failed to reveal the means whereby the Warlord and his mate re-turned to Barsoom, nor is the fate of U Dan known.

U-Dor: {CM/10-17} Dwar of the 8th Utan of O-Tar, Jeddak of Manator. It was he who captured Tara of Helium and Ghek the kaldane. He chose to oppose Gahan of Gathol in a game of Jetan, with Tara of Helium as one of the Princesses—a decision which cost him his life.

U-Kal: {CM/16-18} A name taken by Gahan of Gathol when masquerading as a citizen of Manataj who wished to play for Tara of Helium at the Jetan Games in Manator.

Ulah: {SM/19-23} A slave girl in the service of Ozara, Jeddara of the Tarids, on Ladan, or Thuria, the nearer moon of Barsoom.

Uldak: {SM/4,5} A member of the Assassins' Guild of Zodanga. He was ordered to kill John Carter, or Vandor, as they knew him; but he met his match and died with the mark of the Warlord on his chest.

Ul-to: {LG-3/13} A member of the palace guard of Hin Abtol, Jeddak of Panar. Called upon to match John Carter in a sword fight, he was easily bested by the Warlord.

Ul Vas: {SM/18-23} The fat, arrogant jeddak of the Tarids, a dying race on Thuria, the nearer moon of Barsoom. He and his followers had the ability to make themselves invisible to others through a form of hypnosis.

Umka: {SM/17+} A Masena, or cat-man, of Ladan (Thuria). Of basic human frame, his fingers and toes were those of an arboreal creature. He had but one eye, in the center of his forehead, his nose was wide and flat, and he had no visible ears. His most remarkable features were his two mouths, one above the other. The larger, lower mouth had a powerful set of teeth which were used with deadly results when fighting. The upper mouth was round and toothless. He had a stiff yellowish mane along the center of his skull. His skin was chameleon-like and changed color to match its background.

A fellow-prisoner of the Tarids with John Carter, he taught the latter the language of the Tarids. Later, he escaped and returned to his home in the jungle.

Ur Jan: {SM/2+} Head of the Assassins' Guild of Zodanga, and an avowed enemy of John Carter. He was a very large man, an excellent fighter and, although not too clever, a strong leader.

He kidnapped Dejah Thoris and fled with her and Gar Nal, in the latter's spacecraft, to Thuria. John Carter followed in Fal Sivas' ship. All were captured by the Tarids, so they joined forces in a successful effort to escape. As a result of their enforced association, Ur Jan came to admire the Warlord and swore fealty to him.

Ur Raj: {SMM/24−29} A red man from Hastor, who had been captured by Amhorites and was placed on exhibition in their zoo. He escaped along with Vor Daj (in the body of Tor-dur-bar) and Bal Tab, a green man.

Uthia: {CM/1,2} A young slave girl in the palace of John Carter, and the personal attendant of Tara of Helium.

U-Thor: {CM/13+} Jed of Manatos, second city of Manator. He is popularly known as the Great Jed−a fact not appreciated by O-Tar, Jeddak of Manator. He married Haja, a captured princess of Gathol, after she was cast off by O-Tar, to whom she had bore a son, A-Kor. U-Thor led an uprising against his jeddak and was happy to see his stepson take over the throne.

U-Van: {CM/12,14} A soldier in the guard of the pits of Manator, whose duty it was to watch the prisoner, Ghek the kaldane.

Vad Varo: {MMM/2+; FMM/F'word; SMM/1,2,6,9} Barsoomian name given to Ulysses Paxton, American, who unexpectedly found himself on the Red Planet after being killed in World War I.

Vaja: {JCM(SMJ)/2-6} A beautiful member of the royal family of Zor. Cousin of Prince Multis Par and sweetheart of U Dan. She was kidnapped by the Morgors of Jupiter, who used her to blackmail U Dan into helping them formulate plans to conquer Barsoom. She escaped from the Skeleton Men, along with Dejah Thoris and U Dan, and fled to Zanor, home of the Savator Zan Dar.

Val Dor: {CM/16+} A soldier of Helium, he fought with John Carter, both against the therns and the First Born, and in Okar. Captured by Manatorians, he was enslaved until picked by Gahan for his Jetan team. He escaped to Gathol in Tara's flier and returned, with troops from Gathol and Helium, to free the royal couple.

Valla Dia: {MMM/3+; FMM/F'word; SMM/1} Beautiful daughter of Kor San, Jeddak of Duhor. She was taken prisoner by troops from Amhor, who lost her to raiders from Phundahl. Here she was sold into slavery and became the property of Ras Thavas, the Master Mind of Mars. Her brain was switched with that of the disfigured jeddara of Phundahl—an operation witnessed by Vad Varo, formerly Ulysses Paxton of the U.S.A. He swore to restore her to her own body, and ultimately did so. They were then married, and now live with her royal father in Duhor.

Vandor: {SM/-} Alias used by John Carter while investigating the Assassins' Guild of Zodanga.

Van-tija: {LG-2/11} The principal wife of Nastor, a dator of Kamtol in the Valley of the First Born.

Vanuma: {SMM/25,26} The first wife of Jal Had, Prince of Amhor. She resented her husband's acquiring Janai as a new wife, so he had her poisoned.

Vas Kor: {TMM/-} A nobleman of Dusar, in the retinue of Prince Astok. Disguised as a slave in the palace of Thuvan Dihn, he made an impression of the key to the controlling destination compass on the aircraft of Carthoris of Helium. He then had himself sold into the staff of the palace of Carthoris, and here he reset the compass just prior to the prince's taking off for Ptarth to assist in the search for the abducted princess of Ptarth. His mission accomplished, he resumed his identity and returned to Dusar to prepare for war against Helium. He attempted to murder Thuvia, when Astok promised to make him a jed, but was killed by Carthoris, posing as Turjun the panthan.

Vobis Kan: {MMM/6-14; SMM/1} Jeddak of Toonol. Hearing that Ras Thavas had revived Gor Hajus, he accused the surgeon of plotting to assassinate him. Sending troops to the Tower of Thavas, he drove Ras Thavas out of Toonol, and later repulsed troops from Phundahl who were attempting to recapture the laboratory.

Vor Daj: {SMM/-} A young padwar in the personal troops of John Carter, he was chosen by the Warlord to accompany him in search for Ras Thavas, the greatest surgeon on Barsoom, because of a terrible injury inflicted on Dejah Thoris in an air collision.

Their destination was Duhor, but due to a faulty compass they landed near the west end of the Great Toonolian Marshes. Here they were captured by a group of synthetic men, or hormads, whom they learned later had been created by Ras Thavas. They were taken to Morbus, an island at the edge of the Marshes, where the man they sought was also a prisoner—of his own creations. Another captive was Janai, a girl from Amhor, a city to the north of Morbus.

Carter and Ras Thavas managed to escape and make their way to Helium, but not before transferring Vor Daj's brain to the body of a giant hormad named Tor-dur-bar. In this new form, the Heliumite fled from Morbus with Janai, only to be captured by Amhorites and placed on exhibition in their zoo. Again he escaped, rescuing Janai from the jed of Amhor. They were picked up shortly after by the War-lord, who was returning to Morbus with Ras Thavas. Vor Daj's brain was restored to his own body, and today he and Janai reside happily in Helium.

Vorion: {JCM(SMJ)/5,6} A Morgor who was thrown into the same cell as John Carter, U Dan, and the Savator Zan Dar, because he had killed a fellow man. He showed no love for his leader, Bandolian, and agreed to help the other three escape. The attempt was made and, along with Dejah Thoris and Vaja, they fled to Zanor in a Morgor ship—except for Carter, who was recaptured. Vorion's ultimate fate has not yet been disclosed.

Wolak: {SM/13} A slave in the service of Fal Sivas of Zodanga. Ordered to kill Vandor, it can be said he tried, but he proved an easy victim for the disguised Warlord.

Woola: *see Part IV, "The Flora and Fauna of Barsoom"*

Xaxa: {MMM/-; SMM/1} Jeddara of Phundahl and High Priestess of Tur. Old and ugly, she purchased the body of Valla Dia, a young Duhorian girl, from Ras Thavas, the great surgeon of Toonol, and had him transfer her brain to the body of the maiden. Some time later, she was kidnapped by Vad Varo, Ras Thavas' assistant (the former Ulysses Paxton of the U.S.A.), taken back to the Tower of Toonol, and her brain restored to its original body. Upon her return to Phundahl, she went mad and died.

Xaxak: {LG-2/6-11} A dator, or prince, of Kamtol in the Valley of The First Born. He purchased John Carter, who was using the name Dotar Sojat, and then matched him against local swordsmen, thus winning large bets. The Earthman's fame soon spread throughout Kamtol and Xaxak wisely saw fit to present his superslave to his jeddak.

Xodar: {GM/7+; WM/1,16; TMM/13; LG-2/4,10} A black dator, or prince, from the Temple of Issus in the Valley Dor. One of the Black Pirates who raided the thern gardens in the Otz Mountains and abducted Phaidor, daughter of the Holy Hekkador.

John Carter boarded Xodar's aircraft and overcame him; however, a larger Pirate ship turned the tables and Carter and Phaidor were taken to the First Born stronghold on the Sea of Omean. Xodar was thrown into prison for having allowed Carter to humiliate him. The two men joined forces with another prisoner — who turned out to be Carter's son, Carthoris — and they escaped to Helium. Xodar helped organize a force that invaded the thern forts and the First Born stronghold. Following the defeat of the Black Pirates and the death of their goddess, Issus, Xodar became jeddak of the First Born and a firm ally of Helium.

Yamdor: {MMM/5,13} The personal slave and bodyguard of Ras Thavas, the Master Mind of Barsoom. A giant of a man, yet graceful and dextrous. It was rumored he was the result of one of the master surgeon's experiments — the body of a man with the brain of a woman.

Yersted: {GM/12,20,21} The First Born officer in charge of the submarine running between the Sea of Omean and the elevator shaft to the Temple of Issus. When captured during the invasion of Omean, he warned John Carter that Issus was prepared for him.

Yo Seno: {FMM/6,7,11} Keeper of the keys of the palace of Haj Osis, Jed of Tjanath. A fat, sensual individual, he was killed by Tan Hadron, who had returned to Tjanath to rescue the two girls, Tavia and Phao.

Zad: {PM/14,15} A giant Thark whom the green woman, Sarkoja, persuaded to challenge John Carter to a duel, on the way from Korad to Thark. After a lengthy battle, Zad was killed, although not before he had almost slain the Virginian, through the connivance of Sarkoja.

Zamak: {SM/18-20} Officer in charge of the guard in the castle of the Tarids on Ladan, or Thuria.

Zanda: {SM/2+} A slave girl in the house of Fal Sivas, scientist of Zodanga. Her father, one of the lesser nobility of Zodanga, was killed when John Carter and his green hordes sacked the city some years earlier.

She was saved by Carter — or Vandor, as she knew him — from Fal Sivas' weird experiments, and accompanied Carter and Jat Or, a young officer in the personal bodyguard of Dejah Thoris, to the nearer moon. No doubt, she and Jat Or were married upon their return to Helium.

Zan Dar: {JCM(SMJ)/4+} A Savator, or blue man, of Zanor, on the planet Sasoom (Jupiter). Imprisoned with John Carter and U Dan in the city of the Morgors, the three escaped with the help of the Skeleton Man, Vorion, and all but Carter fled to Zanor in a stolen aircraft.

Zat Arrras: {GM/16-20} A Zodangan nobleman who was appointed jed of Zodanga when it became part of the Heliumatic Empire, after its capture by John Carter and his green hordes. He became regent of the empire when both Tardos Mors and Mors Kajak were leading expeditions in search for Carthoris. When Carter returned from the Valley Dor, he was thrown into prison by Zat Arrras, but eventually he escaped and led an invasion to the land of the First Born. Pursued by that part of the Heliumatic fleet still loyal to the regent, he was forced into a battle over the frozen wastes of the southern ice field. Those ships under Zat Arrras transferred their loyalty to Carter, and the Zodangan leaped overboard to his death.

Zithad: {GM/12; LG-2/12} Dator of the guard in the Temple of Issus, at the time of the futile uprising of the slaves led by John Carter and Carthoris.

Years later, when Zithad was visiting the court of Doxus, Jeddak of Kamtol, he was asked to uphold the honor of the First Born in a duel with a common slave. The slave, however, was John Carter who easily slew the arrogant black.

Zuki: {SMM/21,22} A man of Gooli chosen to fight the hormad Tor-dur-bar, who with Janai of Amhor had entered the village while fleeing from Morbus. He proved to be quite harmless, better at running than fighting.

Zu Tith: {JCM(SMJ)/2} The former jed of Zor, a city south of Helium and just outside the boundaries of the empire. Because of his tyrannical rule, Helium invaded and annexed the city. Zu Tith was slain in the fighting.

Chapter IV – The Flora and Fauna of Barsoom, Including a Dictionary of Barsoomian Plants and Animals

The Plant Life of Barsoom

John Carter's description of plant life on Barsoom is rather brief and, indeed, vague. He writes of the moss or lichen that covers almost the entire surface of the planet, excluding the polar regions. He mentions trees, but names only half a dozen. He refers to shrubs, grasses, vines, and weeds with little, if any, detail. There is frequent mention of flowers, but we learn little about them except that they are beautiful and of indescribable colors.

That deep canyon on the banks of the River Syl, known as the Valley Hohr, is the home of trees and plants which survived the great drought but which no longer exist on the upper surface of Barsoom. The sun's rays pouring into this narrow valley, together with the abundance of water, have succeeded in maintaining a prehistoric paradise that would be a joy to any Barsoomian botanist.

Jovian plants suffer from the same vagueness. We are told that, on Jupiter, the foliage is deathly pale, due to the lack of sunlight; and that most of the trees and shrubs are living, carnivorous entities, with a nervous system, a brain, and a voice, although apparently they are immobile because of their root system. Reference is also made to a bamboo-like shoot that is wholly vegetable, and to the umpalla—a slender, leafless plant.

The Animal Life of Barsoom

In the animal world, Carter mentions only about twenty different species on Barsoom, and some of these quite briefly. He goes into detail in only a few instances; for example, he provides very little description for such common animals as the Zitidar and the orluk.

We are told (PM/3) that but one mammal exists on Barsoom, and that there are absolutely no hoofed animals. Carter implies that fur-bearing creatures exist in the south polar regions, but fails to name or describe them. We only know that Tars Tarkas was sent south "to make war upon the natives there and despoil them of their furs" (PM/15). When returning to Dor with Xodar, Carter remarked that they were "too far south for the great fur-bearing animals" (GM/8).

We are told of birds and fish, of insects and spiders, of reptiles and snakes, as well as creatures for which no clear description is given. And how does one catalog the winged creature of Ladan, or the carnivorous trees of Jupiter?

None of the animals in the forests of Thuria, the nearer moon of Barsoom, are named and only one is described in any detail. It is four-legged, its skin is scaled like that of a fish, its beak and comb give it a bird-like appearance, and it has membranous wings. Apparently it is about the size of a cat or a rabbit. Other life-forms of Ladan are merely referred to as hunting beasts, as flesh-eaters too large to climb a tree, and as "a veritable diapason of horror" (SM/24).

The creatures of Sasoom, or Jupiter, are not given names but are referred to as being of a hideous, unearthly appearance, both powerful and voracious. Mention is also made of smaller, edible animals and game birds. The Morgors have domesticated certain Jovian animals, we are told, among them an enormous, repulsive-looking creature much like a gigantic centipede—with a fish-like head, a mouthful of sharp teeth, and hooves on all its many feet. It was the Morgor beast of transportation, as many as ten to twelve riding on its long back.

In the following "dictionary" I have not only listed the plants and animals with Barsoomian names but have included those for which only Earth names are supplied. Some entries cover a general category, others are quite specific. References given are not intended to guide the reader to each and every spot where the subject is mentioned, but rather to furnish enough information to properly identify it.

A Dictionary of Barsoomian Plants and Animals

apes: *see white ape.*

apt: {WM/8;SMM/24; LG-3/11} A white-furred beast of the northern polar regions. Its head is like that of a hippopotamus — large, and with a tremendous mouth, but with a pair of horns growing downward from the lower jaw. The eyes are large, reaching from the top of the head down to the lower jaw, and are made up of several thousand ocelli each. Each ocellus has its own lid, and the apt has independent control of as many as he wishes — a few for use in bright sunlight and snow, or many for the dark caves which are its home. It has a pair of arms extending forward from the shoulders. These terminate in hands with which it seizes its prey. The apt stands six to eight feet at the shoulder, and its fur is highly prized for garments and throws. At one time, the Okarians considered the apts sacred and forbade hunting and killing them.

banth: {GM/3} The lion of Barsoom. A savage beast of prey roams the dead sea bottoms. It is almost entirely hairless, having only a tawny mane about its neck. Its hide is yellow and it has a powerful tail. Its long, lithe body is supported by ten powerful legs; its enormous jaws are equipped with several rows of long, needle-like fangs; its mouth reaches to a point far back of its tiny ears; and its enormous, protruding eyes of green add the last touch of terror to its awful aspect. Banths roam singly or in packs. They have a low, moaning cry when hunting, and a terrifying roar for paralyzing their victims.

birds: {PM/21;GM/1;SMM/3} Birds of Barsoom are quite unlike those of Earth. They are brilliantly feathered, apparently are voiceless, and they seem to inhabit only the forested areas, thus posing no problems to the agricultural lands along the canals. Only one type, the malagor, is mentioned by name; and it was thought to be extinct until discovered recently in the heart of the Great Toonolian Marshes.

calot: {PM/4,5; WM/3,5; MMM/8} The Barsoomian dog. About the size of a Shetland pony, with a head somewhat like a frog's, and ten short legs. Its jaws are equipped with three rows of long, sharp tusks. Faster than an Earthly greyhound, it is the fleetest animal on Barsoom. Highly intelligent, it is loyal to its master, a ferocious fighter, and has tremendous endurance. It is omnivorous, although mainly a meat-eater. Domesticated by the green men, it is used as an individual watchdog or in packs to guard the herds and camps.

calot tree: {WM/5} A carnivorous plant about the size of a large sagebrush. Each branch ends in a set of strong jaws, capable of seizing and eating large beasts of prey. Carter does not give the range of growth of this repulsive tree, but it does thrive in the Kaolian Forest — which suggests a tropical nature.

darseen: {PM/21; SM/17} A chameleon-like reptile, inasmuch as it can change color at will. No further information is available concerning this creature.

fish: {FMM/7; SMM/19} Fish are rare on Barsoom, which is an almost waterless world. They are found in the underground rivers, in the lakes of the Great Toonolian Marshes and, no doubt, in the Valley of the First Born, the Lost Sea of Korus, and the Sea of Omean (although there is no mention of them being used by the First Born). Tan Hadron and Nur An did not appear astounded when they found fish in the river beneath Tjanath, nor did they hesitate to eat them.

gloresta: {SMM/3} One of the flowering plants that grow in profusion in almost any depression that holds even the slightest trace of moisture.

grass: {WM/5} Carter mentions a slender, purple grass that grows to a height of eight to ten feet and bears red-and-yellow fronds. It is found in low-lying equatorial areas.

insects: {WM/5; FMM/16; SMM/3,23} Barsoom harbors a wide range of insects—from dainty, beautiful creatures that move silently from flower to flower, to giants with a wingspread well over thirty feet. Some of the latter species have powerful jaws and deadly stingers and can easily best small reptiles. There is no mention of Barsoomian bees, but we do know that honey is produced, particularly in Dusar. However, due to lack of any evidence, we are unable to state whether it is made by insects or simply from plants.

Komal: {TMM/9-12} A huge banth that was worshipped by the Lotharians. Subdued by Thuvia of Ptarth through her uncanny ability to control these animals, it aided her in escaping from Lothar, and died defending her from a band of green savages.

lawns: {PM/21; TMM/3} The lawns of Barsoom are a bright scarlet moss or lichen. The color is likely due to sufficient moisture for the plant to produce the red tone. Where such moisture is not plentiful, the growth either fades to a yellow color or is replaced by a similar type of moss of the latter hue.

lizards: {FMM/7} The only lizard appearing in the chronicles is the one encountered by Tan Hadron and Nur An on the banks of the River Syl, beneath the city of Tjanath. It is described as a great white creature with gaping jaws large enough to engulf a man at a single swallow.

malagor: {SMM/3,19} A giant bird, long thought to be extinct. It was discovered by Ras Thavas and his followers near the ancient, deserted city of Morbus, within the Great Toonolian Marshes. Many of them were captured, domesticated, and used as aerial transport by the hormads. Each bird is capable of short flights with two persons, or of longer trips with only one rider.

man-flower: {WM/5} A creeper or vine found in the Kaolian Forest. Its blooms have eyes and hands with which to see and seize the insects which form the plant's diet.

mantalia: {PM/20; FMM/4; LG-1/13} A shrub or tree which grows to a height of eight to twelve feet and in groves of varying sizes. It is found scattered over the dry seabeds of all but the polar regions. This plant furnishes a plentiful supply of milk, which it manufactures from the soil, the air, and the rays of the sun. A single plant, when tapped, will give eight to ten quarts of milk a day.

man-tree: {JCM(SMJ)/8,9} A living, carnivorous plant found in the jungles of Sasoom. (Han Du called it an animal.) It has a nervous system, a brain, and possibly speech, although this has not been proven.

The limbs of this tree writhe and twist, searching out a victim and seizing it in a snake-like embrace. At the end of its stem is a huge blossom containing a many-toothed mouth and two lidless eyes. The smaller plants devour insects; the larger catch and eat animals, even large beasts of prey. The branches of these trees, when sliced and roasted, make an excellent meal, tasting much like veal.

moss: {PM/3,15} The ocher or yellow lichen which covers the dead sea bottoms of Barsoom, as well as the hills and lower plateaus. Herbivorous animals, such as the thoats and zitidars, can live almost indefinitely upon this moss, for it holds in its tiny stems sufficient moisture to meet the limited demands of these animals.

orluk: {WM/8,9} A fur-bearing animal of the polar regions, and one highly prized for its magnificent black-and-yellow-striped coat. We are given little information about this creature, except that it is an "elephantine beast of prey" (WM/9).

pimalia: {GM/6; TMM/1; CM/22; FMM/1; SMM/3} A flowering shrub of great beauty found in almost every Barsoomian garden, as well as in its wild state in depressions among the hills. Its large blooms are among the most beautiful of flowers. It produces an oil which is used as a body lotion by the women of Barsoom.

plant men: {GM/1} One of the original life-forms that came direct from the Tree of Life and which have not changed over the past twenty-three million years. The adult plant man stands ten to twelve feet tall and is of a general human shape but with short, sinuous arms much like an elephant's trunk. It also has a massive tail some six feet long. Its body is hairless and of a ghoulish blue color except for a broad band of white that encircles the single, protruding eye—an eye that is all dead white: pupil, iris, and ball. The nose is a ragged, inflamed, circular hole in the center of a blank face. There is no mouth in the head, which is covered by a tangled mass of jet-black hair, each strand of which looks like a live earthworm. The feet are flat, broad, and about three feet long. It eats through two mouths, one each at the end of the serpentine arms.

The young of these repulsive creatures start as a swelling in the armpits, which burst into buds, which in turn develop into tiny replicas of the parent, suspended by a cord from the armpit to the head of the infant. When they reach ten to twelve inches in length, the cord breaks and they become independent entities. Plant men move about in great leaps of twenty to thirty feet, much like our own kangaroos; in fighting, they leap over their opponents and slash down at them with their powerful tails.

reptiles: {GM/4,13; WM/3; SMM/23; FMM/7} Reptiles are rare upon Barsoom, although they common in the early days of the planet. They are hideous creatures, indescribably repulsive and venomous, and there is nothing on Earth with which to compare them. A few survivors of this genus still can be found in the interior of the Great Toonolian Marshes. In the depths of the Lost Sea of Korus are water reptiles known as silians. (There are also known to be great lizards in underground caverns.)

rykor: {CM/6} At first, a burrowing animal domesticated by the kaldanes and trained as a hunting steed.

Later, the kaldanes took over full command of the creature's faculties, even forcing it to walk erect. Needing only its sense of taste to survive, its head was reduced to nothing more than a mouth, and the kaldane rode on its neck, controlling the beast by attaching tentacles to its spinal column. In order to improve the rykor's physical structure, the kaldanes crossed it with captive red men and eventually came up with a powerful and beautiful mode of transportation which they could abandon when it became ill or injured.

silian: {GM/4,13} A slimy, repulsive water creature found in the Lost sea of Korus, in the Valley Dor. Therns believe that, when a man dies before his allotted time of one thousand years, his spirit passes into the body of a plant man. Should the plant man be killed before the thousand years are up, his soul passes on into a white ape; and, if there is still time left when the ape dies, the soul passes forever into the body of a silian.

sith: {WM/5} An almost-extinct giant insect found in the Kaolian Forest. It resembles a bald-faced hornet about the size of an ox. It has powerful jaws, a mighty, poison-laden stinger, myriad-facet eyes covering three-quarters of its face, and it can move with lightning-like speed in any direction. Its venom has certain commercial uses and is the best weapon against the sith itself.

skeel: {GM/8; TMM/2; FMM/9; SMM/3; LG-4/2} A tall, drought-resisting tree, upon which it is said the civilization of Barsoom was erected. Its fine, hard wood is used in making floors, doors, and many other wood products capable of lasting for centuries. The tree bears large, delicious nuts and is popular, in groves, for parks and large gardens.

snakes: {WM/3} Mentioned only once in the Warlord's records. Loathsome, venomous, crawling creatures beyond Earthly terms of description. Carter encountered them deep in the passageways beneath the Otz Mountains.

somp: {LG-4/2} The fruit of the sompus tree. It is citrus-like, with a thin, red rind. The pulp resembles grapefruit but is much sweeter, and is considered a great delicacy.

sompus: {LG-4/2} The tree which produces the delicious pulpy fruit known as somp. It is cultivated widely along the canals and grows wild in tropical valleys such as the Forest of Lost Men.

sorak: {PM/14; LG-2/7} A household pet about the size of a small cat. It has six legs, and teeth; but we are not told if it is a fur-bearing animal or smoothskinned like a calot.

sorapus: {GM/8; WM/2; TMM/1; FMM/1} A hardwood tree used in the making of wall panels and furniture. The wood has a beautiful grain and takes a high polish. A garden favorite, with widely spreading branches and gorgeous blooms of varying hues. It bears a great hard-shelled nut that contains a most succulent meat.

spiders: {FMM/7} On Barsoom, large insects with twelve legs that grow upward from the spine. They travel by clinging to overhead gossamer webs. If dislodged, they lie helpless on the ground, legs waving futilely. Very likely poisonous, they also have cruelly fanged mouths. Their webs can be woven into the strongest of cords and into a fabric of unbelievable lightness and strength, which will hold water and is almost impossible to tear.

subterranean plants: {FMM/7} Weird, grotesque, almost colorless shrubs with strange, angular, brittle branches and indescribable blossoms. They grow along the banks of Barsoom's rare underground rivers and streams.

thoat: {PM/3,8,15,20; GM/15} The Barsoomian steed. The giant thoat used by the green men "towered ten feet at the shoulder; had four legs on either side; a broad flat tail, larger at the tip than at the root, and which it held straight out behind while running; a gaping mouth, which split its head from its snout to its long, massive neck... it was entirely devoid of hair, but was of a dark slate color and exceeding smooth and glossy. Its belly was white, and its legs shaded from the slate of its shoulders and hips to a vivid yellow at the feet. The feet themselves were heavily padded and nailless" (PM/3). The thoat can live almost indefinitely without water, getting sufficient moisture from the moss that covers so much of the surface of Barsoom—and is also its main source of food. The rider guides his mount by telepathic means, using neither bridle nor reins. A form of saddle is employed, sometimes with elaborate trappings and blankets.

The red Barsoomians have domesticated a small, gentle thoat about the size of a horse. In color and shape it is an exact replica of its huge and fierce cousin. Some nations raise thoats for food as we would beef cattle. The rare albino thoat is highly prized, one that only a jeddak should ride.

trees: {GM/1,9; LG-4/2} Trees of Barsoom are a relatively rare and highly valued commodity. They are found in sunken, tropical basins where water is available, and in the Valley Dor—that great depression at the south pole which also contains the Lost Sea of Korus. Here will be found forest giants a hundred feet in diameter and reaching over a thousand feet into the sky. Their smooth, glossy bark ranges in color from ebony-black, through ivory, to white as the finest china. Others are azure, scarlet, yellow, and deep purple. The foliage is bright and multi-colored, as are the blooms, which appear upon the branches. The forests of equatorial Barsoom consist mainly of skeel, sorapus, and sompus trees. The first two are nut-bearing hardwoods and the sompus produces a sweet, citrus-type fruit.

ulsio: {CM/12; LG-1/5} The Barsoomian rat. This rodent "is a fierce and unlovely thing. It is many-legged and hairless, its hide resembling that of a new-born mouse in repulsiveness. In size and weight it is comparable to a large Airedale terrier. Its eyes are small and close-set, and almost hidden in deep, fleshy apertures. But its most ferocious and repulsive feature is its jaws, the entire bony structure of which protrudes several inches beyond the flesh, revealing five sharp, spadelike teeth in the upper jaw and the same number of similar teeth in the lower, the whole suggesting the appearance of a rotting face from which much of the flesh has sloughed away" *(CM/12)*. It is a burrowing creature, living in colonies in basements and dungeons beneath the cities, and in self-made tunnels.

umpalla: {JCM(SMJ)/9} A Jovian plant or shrub used by the Savators of Han Du's city to mark the location of their homes, which are coated with the sand of invisibility. It is a simple, leafless stock a foot or two tall and bearing a single, fuzzy blossom at its top.

unknown creatures: {PM/18,20; GM/14; WM/5; SM/17,24} Frequent mention is made of creatures for which no clear description is given—such as strange, uncouth monstrosities with vicious fangs and hairy faces.

Twice John Carter encounters such mysterious beasts in the pits of the Warhoons. It is possible these were ulsios, beasts with which he had had no previous contact. Nor are the savage, roaring man-eaters of the Kaolian Forest identified; nor the hunting beasts of Ladan (Thuria), in the jungle across the river from the castle of the Tarids.

usa: {CM/3} A fruit tree common throughout Barsoom. It requires little irrigation and bears abundantly. "The fruit, which ranks high in food value, is one of the staple foods of the less well-to-do, and because of its cheapness and nutritive value forms one of the principal rations of both armies and navies upon Barsoom, a use which has won for it a Martian *sobriquet* which, freely translated into English, would be, The Fighting Potato" *(CM/3)*.

white ape: {PM/6; GM/2; MMM/3; FMM/3} A colossal, ape-like creature, white and hairless except for an enormous shock of bristly fur upon its head. It stands from ten to fifteen feet in height, has an intermediary set of limbs (arms) midway between its upper and lower limbs. The eyes are close together and non-protruding; the snout and teeth are much like that of an African gorilla. The white apes are tribal by nature; they have a spoken language; they carry clubs; and some even wear strips of hide in imitation of the harness of the green men. Their homes are the deserted cities scattered across the planet.

Woola: {PM/4-6; GM/-} A calot, or Barsoomian watchdog, in the retinue of Tars Tarkas. He was given the task of guarding John Carter. From this grew as strong a bond as is possible between man and beast. This loyal creature more than once almost gave his life in defense of his master.

worms: {GM/7; LG-2/12} Sixteen-legged creatures which occupied one of the four sections of the large nuts which grew on the Tree of Life. Eventually freed from their shell, they, along with the white apes and renegade black men, were the progenitors of all forms of animal life on Barsoom.

Zitidar: {PM/7,15; WM/6; SMM/24} A huge mastodonian beast used as a draft animal by the green Barsoomians. Its master uses neither bridle nor reins, but guides it solely by telepathic means. Zitidars are raised by some red nations, for their flesh and hides; and a few, Ptarth for one, use them as draft animals. They are hairless, with padded feet, and are herbivorous, living on the ochre moss that covers most of Barsoom. No clear physical description of these animals is contained in the chronicles (which stress only their tremendous size).

Chapter V – Measurements on Barsoom—Linear, Time, Monetary—and a List of Barsoomian Numbers

Burroughs has furnished the Mars series with three tables: linear, time, and monetary. A study of all three is warranted, particularly the first two.

Linear Measurement

One of the most confusing features encountered in the sagas is that of the measurement of distance. It would appear that Carter was not too clear in his notes when drawing up a "Table of Linear Measurement" (*TMM/6*), and this was further compounded by Burroughs when setting down the adventures of his wandering uncle.

Chapter 6 of *Thuvia, Maid of Mars* contains a footnote which gives the following table:

10 sofads = 1 ad
200 ads = 1 haad
100 haads = 1 karad
360 karads = 1 circumference of Mars at the equator.

And goes on: "A haad, or Barsoomian mile, contains about 2,339 Earth feet. A karad is one degree. A sofad about 1.17 Earth inches."

The lines in the list above are correct—as far as they go—but the haad equaling 2339 feet, and the sofad equaling 1.17 inches are miscalculations, owing to a missing term—the "sof." As one example: if a sofad is 1.17 inches as stated, then a haad would be 2339 *inches*, not *feet*.

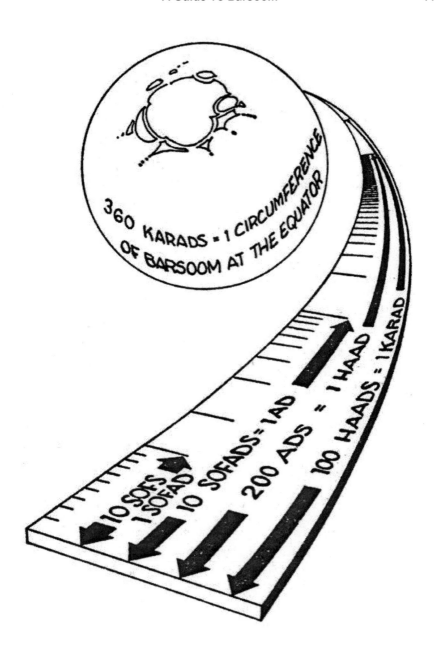

360 KARADS = 1 CIRCUMFERENCE OF BARSOOM AT THE EQUATOR

100 HAADS = 1 KARAD

200 ADS = 1 HAAD

10 SOFADS = 1 AD

10 SOFS = 1 SOFAD

The Barsoomian "Table of Linear Measurement" *should* read:

10 sofs = 1 sofad
10 sofads = 1 ad
200 ads = 1 haad
100 haads = 1 karad
360 karads = 1 circumference of Barsoom at the equator.

It is the *sof* that equals 1.17 inches, and so we have the following table of conversion:

1 sof = 1.17 inches
1 sofad = 11.694 inches (the Barsoomian foot)
1 ad = 116.94 inches = 9.75 feet
1 haad = 23388.00 inches = 1949 feet

Thus: 2.71 haads to the mile.

This is supported by information contained in Chapter 2 of *A Fighting Man of Mars*; i.e., (1) a haad being 1949.0592 Earth feet, and (2) an ad is about 9.75 Earth feet.

To establish the "sof" one must turn to Chapter 12 of *Swords of Mars*, where we read that human beings on Thuria would, in proportion to their environment, be *about 9 1/2* inches tall — or, in Barsoomian terms, 8 sofs tall. Thus: 1 sof equals *about* 1.19 inches (or, to be exact, 1.17 inches).

One can assume that Burroughs thought "sof" was merely an abbreviated form of "sofad" and therefore left it out of the table in *Thuvia, Maid of Mars* and then went on to credit the sofad with the 1.17 inches. It wasn't until later on in his writings that he corrected this error, which was no doubt discovered during discussions between Burroughs and Ulysses Paxton when the latter was transmitting the tale of Tan Hadron of Hastor to Earth via the Gridley Wave (*FMM/F'word*).

Time Measurement

The Barsoomian day is approximately 24 hours and 37 minutes long—Earth time. Their day starts at the equivalent to our 6:00 a.m. and is divided into 10 equal parts. These are divided further into 50 shorter parts, each of which is broken down into 200 parts—each of these roughly equivalent to our own "second." The Barsoomian "Table of Time" reads (footnote, *GM/16*):

200 tals = 1 xat
50 xats = 1 zode
10 zodes = 1 revolution of Mars upon its axis

Converting this to Earth time, we have the following table:

1 tal = .885 of a second
1 xat = 2.95 minutes
1 zode = 2 hours, 28 minutes

Or, as we are told in Chapter 2 *of A Fighting Man of Mars,* a zode equals 2.462 hours.

All this seems quite clear until we encounter another dissertation on Martian time, given by Carter when speaking of his plans to escape from Invak in the Forest of Lost Men *(LG-4/11).* He says, "A Martian day is divided into ten zodes, there being four tals to a xat, or two hundred to a zode." This certainly contradicts the table appearing in the footnote in Chapter 16 of *The Gods of Mars,* quoted above.

Thus, we have a tal equaling .885 seconds in the first table and 44.25 seconds in this new table. I favor the earlier record, for, if we turn to Chapter 3 of *The Warlord of Mars,* to the part where Carter is unlocking a door by means of light rays, we will read that he let the light shine for 50 tals, for one xat, and for 25 tals. "Those last twenty-five tals were the longest twenty-five seconds of my life," he says as he counts them off. Such a countdown would not be likely if each tal were three-quarters of a minute in length. This opinion is further strengthened by a statement made by Carter only moments before he describes the clock. In *Llana of Gathol*, Book 4, Chapter 10, we read, "A tal is about eight tenths of an earthly second."

To solve the mystery of the later table, I suggest we coin a Barsoomian word for that period of time 44.25 seconds long. Let us call it a "tak," and revise the table accordingly.

1 tal = .885 seconds
50 tals = 1 tak = 44.25 seconds
4 taks = 1 xat = 2.95 minutes
50 xats = 1 zode = 2 hours, 28 minutes

While on the subject of time, one might wonder how Barsoomians divide their year. Burroughs uses the terms "month" and "week," and he has Carter speaking of his ten years on Mars—i.e., 1866-1876— whereas the Barsoomian calendar would show only 5.3 years. Also Carter uses the phrases "ten long years," "ten long Earth years," and "ten years" when speaking with Tars Tarkas in the cave in the Golden Cliffs (GM/2). During the same conversation, the green warrior says he started on his journey down the Iss a "month since." In Chapter 8 of *The Gods of Mars*, Carthoris speaks of his mother mourning for ten long years. In Chapter 16 of the same book, Kantos Kan uses "month" and "weeks" when referring to the expedition that went in search of Carthoris.

Burroughs defends his use of the Earthly equivalent rather than the Barsoomian terms (Footnote, *GM/ 16*), but I fear he became some-what confused—as did Carter himself. When thrown into prison by Zat Arrras, the Virginian counted off 330 days and thought that al-most a year had passed (*GM/19*). He did not realize his error until af-ter talking with the dator, Yersted, commander of the submarine at Dor (GM/ 20).

In Chapter 1 of *The Warlord of Mars*, we are told, "...six long Mar-tian months" have passed, giving us the impression it was half a year—although there is nothing to show that Barsoom has a twelve-month year. I feel this was a hybrid expression, part Barsoomian, part

Earthly. Earth uses the revolutions of her moon to arrive at a twelve-month year, but in no practical way can Barsoomian months be figured from either of her two satellites. However, in *Llana of Gathol*, Book 3, Chapter 3, Carter mentions that a Barsoomian month is "about seventy days of Earth time." If converted, this would be *about* 68 Barsoomian days.

A Barsoomian year is 687 Earth days long, but is only 668.6 Martian mean solar days. (Thus, Carter erred even further when counting the days of Dejah Thoris' captivity in Dor, referred to above.) If the customary Barsoomian decimal system is used, the year would be divided into ten parts of 67 days each, with minor adjustments from time to time — like our own leap year — to even things out.

The late Frank J. Brueckel, one of Burroughs' keenest fans, retired from the Hale Observatory (Mt. Wilson and Palomar), suggested that the Barsoomian calendar could be arranged in five-year cycles — a cycle containing two "short years" of 668 days each and three "long years" of 669 days each. A "short year" would have eight "long months" each of 67 days, and two "short months" of 66 days each. A "long year" would have nine 67-day months and one 66-day month.

Continuing with the decimal system, each month could have 10 "weeks" (or 9+) of 7 days each; or it could have 7 "weeks" (or 6+) of 10 days each. Unfortunately, this matter will never be resolved until such time as those vital documents given by the Warlord to his nephew are recovered from the International Astronomic Society, where they seem to have been reposing for the past seventy years or more (Footnote, *GM/16*).

The following table was found recently among ERB's notes:

10 zodes = 1 padan (day)
67 padans = 1 teean (month)
10 teeans = 1 ord (year)

These Barsoomian terms — "padan," "teean," and "ord" — are not used in any of the eleven tales but do appear on Burroughs' worksheet "Characters, etc. in GODS OF MARS."

Barsoomians have the wristwatch, as will be noted in Chapter 3 of *The Warlord of Mars*, where Carter describes the "Barsoomian chronometer" that he wore in a bracelet of gold about his wrist. It is, he says, "a delicate instrument that records the tals and xats and zodes of Martian time, presenting them to view beneath a strong crystal much after the manner of an earthly odometer." It could be assumed that this timepiece bore one hand for the zodes, one for the xats, and a "sweep hand" for the fleeting tals. However, I feel it would be most difficult to distinguish 10,000 tals imprinted on the circumference of even a two-inch watch face, especially when attempting a "count-down." Thus, I suggest a digital-type face with three windows showing (1) the zode, (2) the xats, and (3) the tals. The tals would be rolling by at the rate of one every .885 of our seconds and could be quite easily counted.

The Barsoomian clock *(LG-4/11) does* have three hands: one for the zodes, one for the xats, and one for the (my) newly named "taks." (Carter uses the term "tal" here, but this is an obvious error, as a tal is .885 of a second and the unit indicated is 44.25 seconds in duration.) The dial of the clock is "marked with four concentric circles; between the inner circle and the next outer one the zodes are marked from one to ten; in the next circle, the xats are marked from one to fifty between each two zodes; and in the outer circle two hundred tals ['taks'] are marked between the radii which pass through the zode numbers and extend to the outer periphery of the dial. Their clock has three different colored and different length hands, one indicating the zode, the second one the xat, and the longest one the tal ['tak']."

This may seem somewhat unusual to an Earthman, for it means a sector of 36° is marked off as one zode in the first circle, fifty xats in the second, and 200 "taks" in the outer circle. As each sector contains all the measurements required for each zode, I can see no reason for more than one hand. As that one hand travels across the arc for zode 1 it ticks off the xats and taks until it passes into zode 2 and begins again.

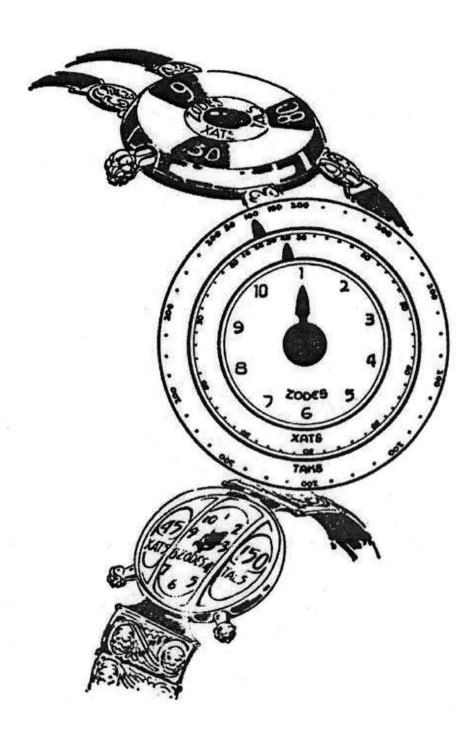

Monetary Measurements

According to *Llana of Gathol*, Book 2, Chapter 11, the Barsoomian "Monetary, or Coinage, Table" would read:

1 bronze pi, comparable to 1 U.S. cent
10 pi =1 silver teepi, comparable to 1 U.S. dime
10 teepi = 1 gold tanpi, comparable to 1 U.S. dollar

These are the only coins in circulation, and they are dull and oval (*TMM/2*). Paper money may be issued by individuals, much as we would write a check, and this must be redeemed twice a year. If the individual should issue more than he can redeem, the government pays his debts and he is forced to work out the amount of indebtedness on the government-run farms or mines (*PM/20* and *LG-2/7,11*).

The above three tables—linear, time, and monetary—are the only ones which appear in the chronicles. Burroughs indicates there are more, but states that they were turned over—with other scientific data—to members of the International Astronomic Society for their perusal and study. Where these priceless documents and papers are now should be a matter of grave concern.

A List of Barsoomian Numbers

Another subject of interest is that of Barsoomian numerals. Little information is available, our main source being those hormads created by Ras Thavas, who were identified by numbers rather than by names (in *Synthetic Men of Mars*). This has helped in drawing up a table, but unfortunately only five hormads are so designated:

Tor-dur-bar = four million eight (*SMM/4*)
Teeaytan-ov = eleven hundred seven (*SMM/4*)
Ay-mad = one man (*SMM/11*)

Il-dur-en = (?) million (?) (*SMM/15*)
Dur-dan = million (?) (*SMM/15*)

Even here we have three unknowns: il, en, and dan. Assuming they are primary numbers, they could be any three of the numbers two, three, five, six, and nine.

The following meager table is all that can be compiled from the data contained in the chronicles, and even it is partially guesswork:

one = ay   as in: *ay*-mad / *one* man (*SMM/11*)

two = ?

three = ?

four = tor   as in: *Tor*-dur-bar / *four* million eight (*SMM/4*)

five = ?

six = ?

seven = ov   as in: Teeaytan-*ov* / eleven hundred *seven* (*SMM/4*)

eight = bar   as in: Tor-dur-*bar* / four million *eight* (*SMM/4*)

nine = ?

ten = tee   as in: *tee*pi / *ten* cents (*LG-2/11*)

eleven = teeay   (ten plus one)

twelve = ?

thirteen = ?

fourteen = teetor   (by presumption)

fifteen = ?

sixteen = ?

seventeen = teeov   (by presumption)

eighteen = teebar   (by presumption)

nineteen = ?

twenty = ?

one hundred = tan   as in: *tan*pi / *one hundred* cents *(LG-2/11)*

one thousand = dar   as in: dar, a unit of one thousand men *(LG-3/4)*

one thousand = mak   as in: umak, a unit of ten thousand men *(FMM/F'word)*

one million = dur   as in: Tor-*dur*-bar / four *million* eight *(SMM/4)*

Chapter VI – The Language, Religions, and Customs of Barsoom

Language

When John Carter was learning the language of the green men of Barsoom, he was quite unaware he was mastering the only language spoken on that world. It was some time later, when conversing with Dejah Thoris in Korad, that she told him, "All Barsoomians speak the same tongue from the ice-clad south to the ice-clad north, though their written languages differ. Only in the valley Dor, where the river Iss empties into the lost sea of Korus, is there supposed to be a different language spoken" (PM/11).

The "different language" was that once spoken by the black-skinned First Born. Apparently it has fallen into disuse, and only on rare occasions do the Black Pirates make use of their mother tongue. Xodar did when calling to the crew of the submarine on the shore of the Sea of Omean (*GM/8*). The most frequently used word from the old tongue is the title "dator," which is equivalent to "prince" or "jed" (GM/7).

Carter elaborates on language while in the Pit of Plenty in Kadabra (*WM/11*). He states: "Martian writing is rather difficult to explain to an Earth man—it is something of a cross between shorthand and picture-writing, and is an entirely different language from the spoken language of Mars.

"Upon Barsoom there is but a single oral language.

"It is spoken today by every race and nation, just as it was at the beginning of human life upon Barsoom.

It has grown with the growth of the planet's learning and scientific achievements, but so ingenious a thing it is that new words to express new thoughts or describe new conditions or discoveries form themselves—no other word could explain the thing that a new word is required for other than the word that naturally falls to it, and so, no matter how far removed two nations or races, their spoken languages are identical.

"Not so their written languages, however. No two nations have the same written language, and often cities of the same nation have a written language that differs greatly from that of the nation to which they belong."

Religions

Burroughs included religion—but not theology—in virtually all his tales, and his Martian series is no exception. In fact, it is one of the best examples of his presumption of the existence of a supreme being. Read, for example, what he says in Chapter 12 of *The Chessmen of Mars*: "We might even walk with God in the garden of His stars while man was still but a budding idea within His mind."

The most widespread religion on Barsoom was the worship of Issus, Goddess of Life Eternal, the supreme deity of Mars. Her home was on the shore of the Lost Sea of Korus in the Valley Dor, a torrid basin at the south pole, completely ringed by the towering Otz Mountains.

The priests of Issus were the white-skinned therns, direct descendants of the ancient Orovars. They dwelt in the honeycombed and highly fortified Otz Mountains and in magnificent palaces on the outer slopes thereof. They also had secret temples hidden in every city and community of Barsoom, from which they spread the word of Issus and kept a finger on the pulse of Barsoom (*GM/13*).

The fanatical therns were led by Matai Shang, Holy Hekkador of the Holy Therns, Father of Therns, Brother of Issus, Master of Life and Death upon Barsoom.

With few exceptions, every nation and every race upon Barsoom were followers of Issus, whether their skins were red, black, or yellow; and even the cruel, loveless green men looked forward to an afterlife in that Elysium at the mouth of the River Iss. Barsoomians believed that when their life expectancy of one thousand years was up, they should take the voluntary pilgrimage down the great Iss to the Valley Dor. As Tars Tarkas described their goal: "...the valley of love and peace and rest to which every Barsoomian since time immemorial has longed to pilgrimage at the end of a life of hate and strife and bloodshed... This, John Carter, is Heaven" (*GM/3*). It was not necessary to wait the thousand years. Anyone could, at any time, make the trip if he or she chose to—and many did.

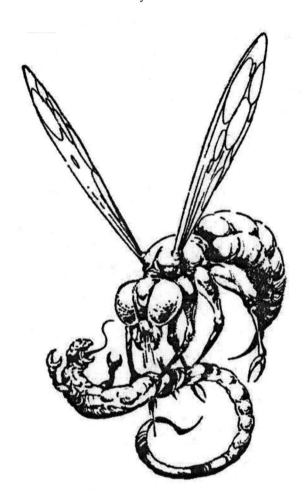

The River Iss—sometimes called the River of Mystery or the River of Death—flows through the southern ice fields, under the Otz Mountains, and into the Lost Sea of Korus. We have no knowledge of its source, its tributaries, its length, or its route as it wends its way southward. Apparently it is an underground stream, without rapids or waterfalls, since the pilgrims—quite unused to any form of water traffic—made their way heavenward in the light, paddle-propelled craft furnished for the purpose by the unseen priests.

I suggest that, although there *is* a River Iss emptying into the Korus, any and all routes taken by those seeking the Temple of Issus also represented, figuratively speaking, the River. Such wayfarers were, quite unknowingly, directed by the thern priests from station to station, along southbound rivers and on land across dead sea bottoms, until they reached a final point of embarkation onto the River Iss itself.

Once one was upon the waters of the Iss, he had no turning back and the dream of Heaven became a nightmare of Hell. Those who changed their minds fled to the Valley of Lost Souls and eked out an existence in pathetic isolation. Those who completed the journey found themselves facing plant men and white apes on the scarlet sward of the Valley Dor. They either met a quick death by these or were enslaved by the ruthless therns nearby. This was the tragic realization of millions of Barsoomians over thousands of years.

The cunning, parasitical therns had no direct contact with their goddess, Issus, but they believed her temple to be the ultimate Heaven, reserved for therns only. This too was a delusion, for Issus—rather than being an omnipotent providence—was nothing more than an ancient hag: a bald and toothless old woman, leader of the haughty black-skinned First Born, who dwelt in the city of Issus and on the subterranean Sea of Omean (although for centuries it was believed they were the dreaded Black Pirates, whose home was said to be on Thuria, the nearer moon).

A long tunnel runs from the Temple of Issus to the main temple of the therns. It was known only to the First Born, who used it to place messages from Issus on the temple altars, much to the mystification of the Holy Therns.

And so the deceitful were, in turn, deceived—and knew it not.

The people of the city-state of Phundahl, on the western edge of the Great Toonolian Marshes, are not followers of Issus. Instead, they worship the Great God Tur, who, they claim, created Barsoom a hundred thousand years ago in his home on the sun. He tossed it out into space and placed life on its surface—man, animal, and plant. The *Tur-*

gan, an impressive tome said to have been written by Tur himself, contains all the facts of life, such as: Barsoom is flat; procreation is a myth, as all life comes from Tur; it is evil to fly or to use telescopes. Anything not found in the *Turgan* is simply not true (*MMM/10*).

Carter found evidence, also, of free thinkers among the Barsoomians. A good example of this is Torkar Bar, Dwar of the Kaolian Road in the great forest of Kaol. This nobleman, of a nation loyal to Issus, told John Carter, "I have questioned and disbelieved the therns and their religion" (*WM/5*).

The Lotharians believe in the power of the mind. They are able to cause things to materialize: food for their sustenance, warriors to battle for them and fade away when their purpose has been served. The etherealists of Lothar maintain that "there is no such thing as matter — that all is mind" (*TMM/7*); whereas the Lotharian realists believe they must perform all the normal functions necessary to human existence, even though the ingredients — such as food and water — are created through a mental process. But even these mental giants, the Lotharians, require a deity. They revered a great banth which they called Komal, and which they declared was the essence of the All. He was the beginning and the end. All life emanated from Komal. Should Komal have ceased to eat, all life upon Barsoom would have ceased to be. Unfortunately, Komal left Lothar with Thuvia of Ptarth and was killed by the Dusarians. What happened to the dwellers of Lothar following this calamity is not told in the chronicles.

Another group of believers in the power of the mind are the kaldanes of Bantoom. Instead of using the brain to create, however, they want to eliminate all but the brain and become nothing more than immobile, pure thinkers. "At the very beginning," they say, "things existed with life, but with no brain. Gradually rudimentary nervous systems and minute brains evolved. Evolution proceeded. The brains became larger and more powerful. In us you see the highest development... The future kaldane will be nothing but a great brain... with nothing to distract it from eternal thought" (CM/5).

The Okarians, secure in their hothouse cities, "had always been known to the Holy Therns and were devout and faithful followers of the ancient cult" (*WM/7*). However, they must have had a substitute for the final pilgrimage down the River Iss, for there were no yellow men in Dor.

Under Salensus Oll, Jeddak of Okar, the great white-furred apts had been deified, and it was forbidden to hunt or kill them. What Matai Shang, the Father of Therns, thought of this form of beast-worship is not known.

There is also a constant indication of ancestor worship by Barsoomians. Dejah Thoris' remark, that she was the daughter of ten thousand jeddaks, and could trace her ancestry straight back to the builder of the first great waterway, is early evidence of this *(PM/13)*. Gahan of Gathol, we are told, "clung... to a certain exalted form of ancestor worship, though it was rather the memory or legends of the virtues and heroic deeds of his forebears that he deified rather than themselves... If there was a life hereafter he knew nothing of it, for he knew that science had demonstrated the existence of some material cause for every seemingly supernatural phenomenon of ancient religions and superstitions" (CM/20). Later (CM/22), we read: "...age is held in great veneration among the peoples of Barsoom, as is true, perhaps, of all peoples whose religion is based to any extent upon ancestor worship." The Manatorians, a backward nation in comparison to the rest of Barsoom, still believe in "Corphals," beings who by seizing control of "the spirits of the wicked dead gain[s] evil mastery over the living" *(CM/13)*. It was believed that they entered only into the bodies of criminals, and could only be killed by the hand of a jeddak.

Customs

In his early wanderings on this strange, new world, Carter soon learned that Barsoomians place a high value on convention, including gallantry and dignity. "Customs have been handed down by ages of repetition," he tells us, "[and] the punishment for ignoring a custom is a matter for individual treatment by a jury of the culprit's peers" (PM/9). And: Even a jeddak cannot set aside the customs of ages *(PM/24)*.

{PM/3} In the Virginian's first encounter with a Barsoomian — the green chief of Tars Tarkas — the latter removed an armlet and offered it to the Earthman. Carter accepted the trinket and placed it upon his own arm: friendship offered, friendship accepted.

{WM/9} Talu, Prince of Marentina, offered an armlet to Carter and Thuvan Dihn when acceptance of his shield, which he had *first* offered, was — quite properly — refused by his rescuers.

{GM/16} To cast your sword at the feet of a fellow Barsoomian is to pledge your loyalty and trust to that person, even though it may cost you your life. To cast it at the feet of a woman means much the same, but can also be interpreted as a declaration of courtship. {LG/1/10} If the recipient is a man, he buckles the sword belt back on its owner; if a woman, she returns the sword, hilt first. Either means the offer of fealty has been accepted. To leave the sword where it lies is to refuse the offer. To return it point first is a complete rejection and an insult. This means a duel then and there, except in the case of a woman — in which event her closest male relative available must champion her.

{PM/13,26; MMM/9} Generally, when two Barsoomians meet each places his right hand on the other's shoulder — the equivalent to our handshake. A stronger show of friendship would be to place both hands on each other's shoulders. Only on rare occasions do Barsoomians actually embrace.

{PM/14; CM/1,2,9} Kissing is permitted on Barsoom, but only between lovers, close relatives, and occasionally one's more intimate friends. A warrior could, under certain circumstances, kiss the hand of his queen; but this is a pledge of loyalty rather than a show of affection.

{GM/8} For a departing gesture or salute, a Barsoomian raises both hands, palms backward, above the head.

{GM/9; TMM/6,7} In ancient Barsoom, some of the more despotic rulers decreed that all persons approaching the throne prostrate themselves. Among the modern nations, the First Born demanded this of slaves and prisoners, but only during the reign of Issus. {WM/1,16; CM/11} Barsoomian troops and other large assemblages honor their leaders or heros by raising their swords aloft and clashing them together. In the ancient city of Manator, the warriors salute their displayed, mummified dead by raising their spears as they ride or march past the silent balconies or shelves.

{PM/21} Instead of receiving a medal for an act of bravery, a Barsoomian warrior is awarded a metal armband for the left arm; and it is usually placed thereon by his jeddak at a public ceremony.

{PM/4} The green men have few formalities, but observe them thoroughly. A warrior will approach his chief, who acknowledges him by name; the warrior replies by uttering the name and rank of his superior. Should two unacquainted green men meet in peace (which is rare), they would quietly exchange ornaments to show their willingness to be friends.

{PM/10,14,18} Among the green men it is the custom, in intratribal quarrels, for the victor to take over the property and women of the vanquished. This also includes the rank, if the victim was his superior. He will also add the latter's surname to his own. Thus, it is obvious that a man with only one name (an "o mad") has won no tribal duels.

{PM/12} When an important prisoner is captured by green men, that prisoner must be taken before their ruler, and it is the responsibility of the leader of the party to see that this is done. Such prisoner can only be killed in self-defense or if he makes an effort to escape. Should he escape, his captor must forfeit his rank.

{PM/10,14; GM/3,7; LG-2/8} Hand-to-hand combat on Barsoom has many rules. The basic code is that the challenged person must defend himself with the same type of weapon as that selected by his opponent, or with a lesser one: Longsword to longsword, dagger to dagger, or shortsword to longsword—if he so chooses—but never a longsword if his assailant has selected a shortsword. To draw one's pistol when challenged with a sword is unpardonable, as is any attempt at foul play. To ask for quarter is considered cowardly, and to offer quarter is often looked upon as a weakness.

{TMM/2} All physically fit Barsoomian men—with the exception of slaves—are considered warriors and must wear martial trappings at all times, no matter what their normal occupation. Only contempt would be shown toward a male Barsoomian who chose to spurn his weapons.

{CM/15; SMM/3} In battle, it is the duty of the officer to *lead* his men rather than *direct* them. For an officer to order a warrior into a situation where he himself feared to go is unthinkable.

{PM/26; GM/20; FMM/15} In the great air battles that take place between nations, it is the custom for a defeated commander to leap to his death rather than surrender with his ship. {LG-3/6} A drunken commander will not be tolerated on board his ship. His own crewmen will throw him overboard and will go unpunished, despite such a drastic show of insubordination. Loyalty to an officer is proportionate only to the responsibility he shows toward his men.

{PM/13,18; GM/17; CM/3} Green men burn their dead in a funeral pyre. Modern red men dress theirs in special trappings before disposing of them. In the red Barsoomian household it is the custom to drape the wedding trappings of the deceased over his or her dining chair, and to have a slave stand in attendance beside it during the period of mourning. {WM/8} Yellow men used to place their deceased in the Carrion Caves, where, in death and decay, they might serve their country and warn away invading enemies. {SMM/26} In the northern nation of Amhor, court etiquette demands a five-day period between death and burial, and twenty-seven days of mourning when the deceased is a member of the royal family.

{CM/15} The notable dead of the nation of Manator are preserved by a special process. Some are shrunken and mummified; others — especially chiefs and great warriors — are embalmed in a most lifelike condition and placed on exhibition.

{GM/12} Trials are presided over by twenty-one judges selected by lot from men of the same class as an accused; i.e., nobility for a noble, warriors for a soldier; etc. His accusers list the acts charged against him. The defendant is then heard, and he has the right to call witnesses on his behalf. Acquittal or sentence is then pronounced by the judges.

{CM/14} In Manator, a person may be judged by the jeddak alone. Such person is permitted to seek advice and counsel in his defense.

{PM/22} As on Earth, a Barsoomian woman reserves the right to change her mind if she so desires; and to say one thing but mean another (in matters concerning the heart).

{PM/14} "The man of Barsoom does not ask personal questions of women, except his mother, and the woman he has fought for and won." So said Dejah Thoris to John Carter *(PM/14)*. {PM/22} If a red man fights for a woman and then asks for her hand, she becomes his "princess." To call her "princess" without indicating he wishes to marry her is demeaning, and shows he considers her no better than a female slave.

{PM/22; TMM/1,14; CM/18; LG-1/13} A man will show his devotion to a woman by placing his sword at her feet. If she rejects him, she leaves it there; but if she returns it, hilt first, she is acknowledging his offer. Should the man then ask permission to call her his "princess" he is, in fact, proposing marriage. Should she accept, she would call him her "chieftain." Once betrothed, a woman must not listen to words of love from another man, nor has another man a right to speak of love to her if he knows she is betrothed. To complicate matters, custom states that a woman may not marry the man who slays her intended husband. As a weeping Dejah Thoris told John Carter, "We are ruled by custom upon Barsoom" (PM/22).

{PM/22} When a Barsoomian girl's promise to wed is recorded and a proclamation issued, such promise cannot be broken. It is more binding than the ceremonies that follow. A woman may not marry the man who kills her husband, even if he does it in self-defense.

{PM/25} For a royal wedding in Zodanga, I refer the reader to Chap. 25 of A Princess of Mars, wherein will be found an excellent description of such a ceremony. The most unique feature is the use of golden collars.

One is locked about the neck of the groom, the other about that of the bride, the two collars being joined by a golden chain. How long the pair remain thus coupled is not disclosed. {CM/22} Chap. 22 of The Chessmen of Mars contains a description of a royal wedding in the ancient nation of Manator. Here the bride stands at the foot of the throne, awaiting the groom, who enters wearing a grotesque, jeweled mask. The two participants are joined in wedlock by a pair of golden handcuffs locked about their wrists. {PM/27; WM/14} There is no indication of the use of such symbolic adornment in John Carter's marriage to Dejah Thoris, nor in the wedding ceremonies of the Okarians, where a royal wedding must be witnessed by no less than fifty nobles of the court.

{WM/11; CM/20} In Okar, ten days of preparation are allotted prior to the nuptials. In Manator, only seven days are required.

{MMM/14} Two American marriage customs were introduced briefly to Barsoomians by John Carter. When Ulysses Paxton and Valla Dia were wed, Carter stood as "best man," and then the couple went to Helium on their "honeymoon."

{GM/14; TMM/1,12; CM/13; SM/1,3} Barsoomian men, both married and single, may possess female slaves in their household, without offense. Red women, whether free or enslaved, are held in high regard, and to defile even the humblest is considered a heinous crime — "...the persons of the royal women of the courts of Mars are held but little less than sacred" (*TMM/1*). While assassination is rife upon Barsoom, and the Assassins' Guilds can be found in almost every center, such killings apply only to men. To murder a woman is unthinkable.

{CM/1} When announcing the entrance of royalty, a guardsman will strike upon his shield with his shortsword and cry out the rank and name, such as: "The Princess comes! Dejah Thoris!" Royalty is always thus announced.

{CM/1} Upon Barsoom "men are judged upon their own merits rather than upon those of their grandsires, even though pride of lineage be great" *(CM/1).*

{FMM/12} Gambling and games of chance are popular with the people of Barsoom, especially among the troops.

{PM/21; GM/16; CM/11,16} Most Barsoomian cities follow an established pattern. Each is strongly walled, with a main gate and several lesser ones. From these gates, streets lead to a central square in the heart of which is located a great temple. The jeddak's palace, lesser palaces, the embassies, and public buildings such as museums and libraries surround the great plaza. Shops and stores occupy certain sectors stretching away from the square, while other sectors are strictly residential. One street runs completely around the city just inside the wall, and it is here that the public inns for the lowly tradesmen and travelers will be found.

{WM/10; SM/1} Public houses, or hotels, on Barsoom offer little privacy other than for married couples. Male guests are housed in one large chamber, around which are scattered small, raised platforms. On these are spread sleeping silks and furs, either the travelers' own or ones rented from the hotel. No meals are served, but there are baths in adjoining rooms. Unaccompanied women are billeted in similar style on the upper levels of the building. Armed guards patrol the male quarters and are within instant call of the female slaves, who keep constant watch over the fairer sex.

Chapter VII – A General Barsoomian Glossary: Terms, Titles, Organizations, Games, Weapons, Buildings, Streets, Etc.

The following is a comprehensive glossary of Barsoomian terms and topics, etc., that do not appear in Parts II, HI, IV, V, VI, VIII, or IX.

Ad: {TMM/6; FMM/2} A Barsoomian measure of length equal to 9.75 Earth feet. Erroneously, it is shown as 11.7 inches in the table listed in *Thuvia, Maid of Mars*. (For clarification, see Part V, "Measurements on Barsoom.")

Aisle of Hope, the: {GM/17; WM/16} A broad aisle up the center of the great hall in the Temple of Reward in Greater Helium. It leads to the Throne of Righteousness.

aluminum steel: {WM/9} An alloy used largely in the construction of all Barsoomian craft.

anthem (of Helium), battle: *see battle anthem of Helium.*

Assassin of Amhor: {SMM/8,9,25} A descriptive title applied to the professional killer Gantun Gur by the people of Amhor.

Assassin of Toonol: {MMM/8-11} A title used by the people of Toonol when referring to Gor Hajus, a popular assassin of that city.

Assassins' Guilds: {PM/21; TMM/12; SM/1} Upon Barsoom, "assassination is a profession... has its guild, its laws, its customs, and its code of ethics; and so widespread are their ramifications that they seem inextricably interwoven into the entire social and political life of the planet" *(SM/1)*. Carter first mentions assassins when describing the city of Zodanga, with its raised houses and sleeping quarters. "Thievery," he tells us, "is practically unknown upon Barsoom. Assassination is the ever-present fear of all Barsoomians..." *(PM/21)*.

When a person of importance hires a bodyguard, such hireling often is expected to serve not only as his protector but also as his personal assassin. These men, known as "gorthans," can kill another man without compunction, but even the most hardened would refuse to assassinate a woman.

Some of the more notorious assassins are looked upon by the common people as national heros, and their organizations often have considerable political power, even though their killings are illegal and are punishable by death.

Atmosphere Plant: *see Part II, "A Geography of Barsoom..."*

Avenue of Ancestors, the: {GM/16} A main thoroughfare in Greater Helium. It runs for five miles from the Gate of Jeddaks to the Temple of Reward.

Avenue of Gates, the: {CM/16} A street which circles the city of Manator just within the outer walls. On it are many inns.

Avenue of the Green Thoat, the: {SM/5} A street in the city of Zodanga. It was here that Vandor killed the assassin Uldak.

Avenue of Jeddaks, the: {LG-1/12} A broad street in Horz. It ran from the palace of the jeddak to the waterfront, where it entered the Avenue of Quays.

Avenue of Quays, the: {TMM/4} (a) A street in Aaanthor, running from the central plaza to the wharves at which the ocean Once lapped. It is lined with monoliths and palaces.

Avenue of Quays, the: {LG-1/12} (b) A street in Horz, which ran along the waterfront, connecting the many wharves.

Avenue of Warriors, the: {SM/8} A street in the city of Zodanga. On it is a restaurant patronized by Vandor and Rapas the Ulsio.

ay: {SMM/11} Barsoomian word for "one." (*E.g.,* ay-mad, or one-man; and teeay, or eleven [ten + one].)

battle anthem of Helium: {WM/14} A national hymn often sung by the women of Helium as their troops departed for battle.

Black Pirates: {GM/5+; LG-2/-} A name given to the black-skinned First Born because of their fierce raids on towns and villages to kidnap young girls. It was erroneously believed that their base was on Thuria, the nearer moon.

Brother off Issus: {GM/7} One of many titles used by the therns when addressing their leader, Matai Shang.

canals of Barsoom, the: {PM/16,20,21; TMM/11} Great man-made waterways which bring water from the polar ice caps to the rest of Barsoom. They are bordered by rich farmlands, groves of tall trees, farm houses, and stables. A broad highway generally parallels the canal.

carborundum aluminium: {GM/8} A light, impenetrable composition extensively utilized in the construction of Martian fighting ships.

Chamber of Mystery, the: {GM/3,10} A rockbound room deep within the bowels of the Golden Cliffs in the Otz Mountains. It was here that John Carter and Tars Tarkas fought for their lives until rescued by the maid Thuvia.

Chamber of Reptiles, the: {WM/8} A large room well along the corridor deep under the Otz Mountains that leads from the River Iss to the Temple of the Sun. Its floor is covered with venomous snakes and loathsome reptiles.

chief: (a) Name applied in a general sense to jeds, princes, and high-ranking officers.

Chief: {CM/17, Appendix} (b) A Jetan piece, distinguished by a diadem with ten jewels. He can move three squares in any direction—

straight, diagonal, or combination. In live Jetan it is the Chief who directs the play.

controlling destination compass: {TMM/1; SMM/2} A navigational instrument invented by Carthoris. The normal Barsoomian compass is one which can be set so that the needle always points to the intended destination. Carthoris improved upon this by attaching an auxiliary device that automatically steers the aircraft along the path pointed out by the compass. Also, it stops the craft over its intended destination and lowers it to the landing area. A warning bell can be set to awaken the sleeping pilot.

Council of the Seven Jeds, the: {SMM/4,5} Seven hormads, created by Ras Thavas, whose brains were superior to those of the other hormads. They overthrew the great scientist, seized control of Morbus, and forced him to transfer their brains to the bodies of normal red men.

Dance of Barsoom, the: {CM/1} All Barsoomian dances are stately and beautiful, but the dance of Barsoom is a wondrous epic of motion and harmony — with no grotesque posturing, no vulgar or suggestive movements. It has been described as the interpretation of the highest ideals of a world that aspired to grace and beauty and chastity in woman, and strength and dignity and loyalty in man.

dar: {LG-3/4} A military unit of one thousand men, corresponding to an Earthly regiment. Its commander is a teedwar.

dator: {GM/7} A word used only by the First Born. It means prince, or chief.

Daughter of the Lesser Moon: {GM/22} One of many titles imposed by the Black Pirates upon Issus, their queen.

Death, the: {FMM/5,6,8} A form of punishment or execution imposed in the city of Tjanath, where the victim is lowered into a pit deep under the jed's palace. Weird, frightening sounds issue from its unknown depths and no one (until Tan Hadron did so) his ever returned after being thrown therein.

Defender of the Holies: {WM/7} A title used when addressing Kulan Tith, Jeddak of Kaol, but likely common to all rulers who followed the religion of Issus.

disintegrating ray: {FMM/5,9+} An invisible ray discovered by the Jaharian scientist Phor Tak. He then invented a rifle capable of discharging this ray, the vibration of which effects such a change in the constitution of metals as to cause them to disintegrate. Adjustments could be made so that the ray would destroy flesh or wood instead of metal.

dur: Barsoomian word meaning "one million."

dwar: {FMM/F'word} (a) A military rank similar to that of an army captain. The commander of a utan, or one hundred men.

Dwar: {CM/2, Appendix} (b) A Jetan piece. There are two of each color, orange and black, and they are identified by their three-feathered headdress. A Dwar can move three spaces straight in any direction or combination of directions.

eighth ray, the: {PM/21} Also known as the ray of propulsion. Barsoomian scientists discovered that each star and each planet throws off a ray from its surface, out into space. They learned how to confine this force of repulsion of gravity and thereby store the eighth ray of Barsoom in their aircraft, and thus they could ride the skies of Barsoom.

equilibrimotor: {MMM/8; LG-3/3} A one-man flying harness. Somewhat like a ship's life belt, it is filled with the eighth Barsoomian ray of sufficient strength to enable a person to float above the ground. Propulsion is by a small radium motor on the back, with controls attached to the front of the belt. Small, adjustable wings enable the wearer to maneuver about.

ersite: {TMM/1; LG-3/12} Barsoomian stone used in the building of benches and tables.

Father of Therns: {GM/7} One of the titles used by Matai Shang, ruler of the therns.

Fields of Jetan, the: {CM/17} A stadium in Manator where live pieces play Jetan on the orange-and-black-squared turf.

Fifth Jed, the: {SMM/10} A member of the Council of Seven Jeds, in Morbus.

Fighting Potato, the: {CM/3} John Carter's description of the staple army diet, the fruit usa.

Fire God: {SM/18,19} A name given to Sol by the sun-worshiping Tarids of Ladan, or Thuria.

First Jed, the: {SMM/10} A member of the Council of Seven Jeds, in Morbus.

First Parent: {GM/7} A name used, at times, when referring to the Tree of Life.

flier: *see ground fliers.*

Flier: {CM/16, Appendix} (b) A Jetan piece, of which there are two on each side. It is identified by a three-bladed propeller. It moves three places diagonal in any direction or combination of directions, and can jump intervening pieces.

Flying Death, the: {FMM/10} A type of torpedo invented by Phor Tak of Jahar. When launched, it will follow and make contact with the object to which it has been attuned. It is set to explode upon contact.

forandus: {FMM/11} The hardest and lightest metal known to Barsoomians. It is used in the making of wall panels.

Fourth Jed, the: {SMM/10} A member of the Council of Seven jeds, in Morbus.

Garden of the Jeddaks, the: {WM/10; TMM/12} An enclosed area of beautiful trees, shrubbery, and flowers within the palace grounds of the jeddak of Okar, in Kadabra.

Gate of Enemies, the: {CM/11+} One of the main gates into the walled city of Manator. It is here the mummified bodies of slain enemies of note are honored by being placed on display.

Gate of Jeddaks, the: {GM/16} The main gate in the walls of Greater Helium. It opens onto the Avenue of Ancestors, which in turn leads directly to the Temple of Reward.

Goddess of Death: {GM/10} One of many titles given to Issus, ruler of the First Born.

Goddess of Life Eternal: {GM/9} One of many titles given to Issus, ruler of the First Born.

Golden Temple of Issus, the: *see Temple of Issus.*

gorthan: {SM/1} Barsoomian word meaning "assassin."

Grand Decennial Games, the: {CM/17} Greatest of the Jetan competitions of Manator, held at ten-year intervals.

Great Ape of Ptarth: {MMM/11} A self-imposed title used by Hovan Du while his brain was in the body of a white ape.

Great Jed: {CM/13} An unofficial title conferred on U-Thor, Jed of Manatos, by the populace.

Great Plaza, the: {LG-2/11} The large, central square in front of the jeddak's palace in the heart of Kamtol.

Great Power, the: {WM/12} A term used by Solan, the Okarian, when speaking of the mighty magnetic tower at Kadabra.

Gridley Wave: {FMM/F'word} A new type of radio wave discovered by Jason Gridley of Tarzana, California. Burroughs used it to communicate with Vad Varo of Duhor, the former Ulysses Paxton of the U.S. Army. It was by this method that Burroughs obtained the story of Tan Hadron of Hastor.

ground fliers: {WM/9; TMM/2; SMM/24; LG-3/11} There are two types of ground fliers, or surface craft, on Barsoom. In the arctic nations of Okar and Panar, the so-called flier is actually a wheeled motor vehicle, the tires of which are simply rubber-like gas bags filled with the eighth Barsoomian ray. They contain just enough buoyancy to give the car traction for steering purposes. A small, propeller-equipped motor drives the vehicle.

The ground flier found in most Barsoomian cities is merely a modified aircraft designed for use in city streets. "For the greater part they skimmed along the surface of the sward, soaring gracefully into the air at times to pass over a slower-going driver ahead, or at intersections, where the north and south traffic has the right of way and the east and west must rise above it" (*TMM/2*).

Guardian of the North, the: {WM/9+} A mighty magnetic tower on the outskirts of Kadabra, capital city of Okar. It was built directly over the north magnetic pole of Barsoom. The steelhulled aircraft of explorers and invaders were irresistibly drawn to the shaft, where they fell—crumpled and broken—to its base. Their crews were either killed or enslaved by their yellow captors.

haad: {TMM/6; FMM/2} A Barsoomian unit of linear measurement, equal to 1949.0592 Earth feet. There are 2.71 haads to the mile. The footnote in Chap. 6 of *Thuvia, Maid of Mars* is in error in this regard.

Hall of Chiefs, the: {CM/11+} A long, wide hall of almost unbelievable beauty in the palace of the jeddak of Manator. On either side, mounted on thoats, are the deceased jeds of the nation, both man and beast perfectly preserved by the great embalming skill of old I-Gos. It is here that the jeddak retires when faced with a momentous problem upon which his *living* advisers could not agree.

Hall of Jeddaks, the: {JCM(SMJ)/1} A conference room in the palace of Tardos Mors. It is here that the illustrious jeddak sits in consultation with his ministers and advisers.

Hekkador: {GM/7} A title used only by the High Priest of the white-skinned therns.

helmets: {PM/3; LG-1/2,5} A rarity on Barsoom. Apparently a popular item of dress among the Orovars of predrought Barsoom. The few remaining members of this race, now living secretly in Horz, wear a headdress consisting of a leather band around the brow, with a strap crossing from left to right and another from front to back. It is highly decorated with carving and jewels. The strap across the brow bears a beautifully carved piece of gold with identifying designs thereon.

Green Barsoomians wear ornaments strapped upon their heads, but no clear description of these has been given. Generally speaking, the red and the black races use no headgear, although the fighting men of the isolated state of Manator have retained the feathered headbands which identify their military ranks.

High Tower, the: {CM/17} Tallest of the turrets over the Fields of Jetan, in Manator.

Holy Therns: {GM/4} A higher caste among the therns, all of whom were priests of Issus, until their false religion was exposed by John Carter.

hormads: *see introduction to Part III, "A Biography of Barsoom..."*

Immortal Race, the: {GM/9} How the First Born described themselves.

invisibility paint: {FMM/10} A paint invented by Phor Tak of Jahar. When applied to an object, it causes the line of vision to pass completely around such object, thus making it invisible.

invisibility pill: {LG-4/4,12} A pellet developed by the people of the Forest of Lost Men. Shortly after swallowing one, the individual is rendered invisible for a period lasting slightly more than ten zodes.

invisibility sand: {JCM(SMJ)/2,9} "A submicroscopic, magnetic sand composed of prismatic crystals" (JCM*[SMJ]*/2). When applied to an object, it causes light rays to bend around that object, thus removing it from a viewer's line of vision.

Issus, the Temple of: *see Temple of Issus.*

jed: Barsoomian word for "king" — of smaller nations — and for "prince," when the country is ruled by a jeddak, or emperor.

jeddak: Barsoomian word for "emperor."

Jeddak's Award, the: {CM/9} Most highly sought of the trophies awarded at the celebrated display of paintings held annually in Helium. It is customary for Tardos Mors himself to make the presentation.

Jeddak's Games, the: {CM/17} The greatest of yearly competitions on the Fields of Jetan, in Manator.

Jeddak's Guard, the: {CM/18} Personal bodyguard for a nation's ruler. An elite body of warriors.

jeddara: {CM/20} Barsoomian word for "empress."

jedwar: {FMM/F'word} The highest of military ranks. A jedwar is responsible only to his jed.

Jetan: {CM/2, Appendix} Barsoomian chess. It is played upon a board of a hundred alternate black and orange squares. There are twenty black pieces and twenty orange. Rules for this game are set out in the Appendix of *The Chessmen of Mars*. In the nation of Manator, the game is played with living pieces in a stadium, and each square is fought for, rather than being simply taken by the party moving onto it.

kadar: {TMM/8} Barsoomian word meaning "guard."

Kalksus: {TMM/13} A swift, well-armed cruiser-transport under the command of Vas Kor of Dusar.

kaor: Barsoomian greeting, similar to our "hello."

karad: {TMM/6} Barsoomian unit of linear measurement equal to one degree of longitude at the equator, or 36.9 miles.

Keeper of the Towers, the: {CM/11,18} The officer in charge of the Towers of Jetan, in Manator. He is also director of the Games, and holds the rank of dwar.

mad: {SMM/11} Barsoomian word for "man." (*e.g.,* ay-mad, or one-man.)

Master of Life and Death upon Barsoom: {GM/7} One of many titles used when referring to the thern leader, Matai Shang.

Master of the Tenth Cycle: {GM/5} A form of address used when speaking to a thern of the Tenth Cycle.

Mother of the Nearer Moon: {GM/10} One of many titles given Issus, ruler of the First Born.

nerve index machine: {LG-2/5} A great, complicated instrument invented by a scientist of Kamtol. He was then assassinated upon orders of his jeddak, Doxus, who took over its control. This machine records an individual's own reflexes and identifies his own nerve index, which differs from that of any other person.

The master machine generates shortwave vibrations which, when tuned to one's individual nerve index, cause a severe paralytic stroke and almost instant death.

Ninth Cycle: {WM/3} The highest rank among the lesser therns, one below that of the Holy Therns.

ninth ray: {PM/20} The primary colors of Barsoom consist of the seven primary colors of Earth plus two others, indescribable to an Earthman. It is the ninth ray which, when isolated, specially treated, and then released, combines with the ether to create the breathable atmosphere of Barsoom.

nolach: {CM/4} A word used by the kaldanes of Bantoom to denote a person in authority. Possibly it means "foreman."

odwar: {FMM/F'word} (a) The second-highest military rank. Commander of a umak, or ten thousand men.

Odwar: {CM/16,17} (b) Former name of a Jetan piece now known as "flier," and still used in those nations where aircraft are unknown. It represents a general with five feathers.

Okar: {LG-3/8} Flagship of the Panarian navy besieging Gathol, and under the command of Phor San.

o mad: {PM/14} A man with only one name. He could win a second name by defeating a chieftain and taking his victim's surname.

ov: Barsoomian word for "seven."

padwar: {PM/19} (a) A military rank below that of a dwar, and equivalent to our lieutenant.

Padwar: {CM/2, Appendix} (b) A Jetan piece — a lieutenant wearing two feathers. He can move two spaces diagonally in any direction or combination of directions.

Palace of Peace, the: {TMM/2} A beautiful building in Ptarth. Its outer walls bear elaborate carvings and mosaics. Within are the offices of the representatives of various foreign powers.

palthon: {MMM/11} A rare and beautiful stone — blood red — in which are traced in purest white nature's most fanciful designs. It takes a beautiful polish and is used in the making of altars, ornaments, and the like.

panthan: {TMM/11} (a) A Barsoomian soldier of fortune. Usually forced to flee their homeland, these fighting men roam the world selling their sword to whoever desires their service. Brave fighters with a buried past, they are notorious gamblers and free spenders.

Panthan: {CM/2, Appendix} (b) A Jetan piece, represented by a soldier with one feather. His move is one space forward, sideways, or diagonally, but not backward. There are eight to a side.

Pedestal of Truth, the: {GM/17; WM/16} A dais or rostrum in the center of a platform known as the Throne of Righteousness, in the Temple of Reward in Greater Helium. It would be equivalent to the witness stand in American courts.

pi: {LG-2/11} An oval-shaped copper coin of Barsoom, comparable to the American one-cent piece.

Pinsar: {MMM/7,8} The smallest flier in Ras Thavas' fleet of three ships.

Pit of Plenty, the: {WM/11} A unique torture chamber in the city of Kadabra in Okar. It was a glass-lined shaft into which the prisoner was lowered. Behind the glass were shelves of appetizing foods and beverages that the victim could view but not reach.

Polodone: *see Part II, "A Geography of Barsoom..."*

Princess: {CM/2, Appendix} A Jetan piece, the capture of which is the main purpose of the game. She wears a diadem with a single jewel. She can move three spaces in any direction, straight or diagonal, and can jump intervening pieces.

Princess of Life Eternal: {GM/7} One of many titles used when referring to the goddess, Issus.

Ruzaar: {SMM/28+} A ship of the fleet of Helium, en route to Morbus to rescue the padwar, Vor Daj, and Janai of Amhor.

sak: {PM/4} Barsoomian word meaning "jump."

Second Jed, the: {SMM/10} A member of the Council of Seven Jeds, in Morbus.

Sixth Jed, the: {SMM/10} A member of the Council of Seven Jeds, in Morbus. (By inference only, as he is not mentioned specifically.)

sof: {SM/12} A Barsoomian unit of linear measurement, equal to 1.17 inches. Ten sofs equal one sofad.

sofad: {TMM/6; FMM/2} A Barsoomian unit of linear measurement, equal to 11.7 inches. The Barsoomian "foot."
Erroneously said to be 1.17 inches in the table in Chap. 6 of *Thuvia, Maid of Mars*. There are ten sofads to an ad.

Song of Love, the: {CM/8} Barsoom's most beautiful melody.

stairs: {CM/4-9; SM/17} Stairs are a rarity on Barsoom since virtually all nations prefer the ramp, or runway, as a means for moving from one level or floor to another. The interiors of most palaces and public buildings were designed to allow the easy flow, not only of pedestrian traffic, but of mounted personnel; thus, high ceilings, wide corridors, and winding ramps made movement from one level to another a simple matter for a thoat and his rider. *E.g.:* "Along the marble corridors Gahan guided his thoat... he followed the runways and passed through the chambers that led to the throne room of O-Tar" *(CM/18).*

In Chap. 4 of *The Chessmen of Mars*, Carter tells us of stairs in the towers of Bantoom, and he goes on to point out that "The stairways themselves were sufficient to cause remark, since in nearly all Barsoomian architecture inclined runways are utilized for the purposes of communication between different levels, and especially is this true of the more ancient forms and of those of remote districts where fewer changes have come to alter the customs of antiquity."

Again, in *Swords of Mars*, Chap. 17, he states: "Such contrivances were new to [Jat Or], as stairways are not used on Mars, where inclined ramps lead from one level of a building to another." The young Heliumatic padwar found it difficult to negotiate the unfamiliar steps in the castle of the Tarids on Ladan, or Thuria, the nearer moon of Barsoom; and it was this that led Carter to explain, "I had once tried to introduce stairways in my palace in Helium; but so many of my household and my friends came near breaking their necks on them, that I eventually replaced them with ramps." There is no question, however, that the Warlord's daughter, Tara of Helium, had mastered the art of walking up and down stairs, as she showed neither surprise nor dismay when faced with them in the Tower of Luud. It is not unreasonable to assume that Carter conducted the experiment in his palace prior to Tara's adventures in Bantoom and Manator, and that they had been removed by the time Jat Or took up service in the palace guard.

For some inexplicable reason (ERB had not yet stressed the difficulty Barsoomians had in navigating stairs) the great Burroughs artist,

J. Allen St. John, portrays this mistrust of Jasoomian architecture in his illustration of Dejah Thoris in *The Chessmen of Mars* (facing page 8, 1st edn., 1922) Here he shows the princess herself descending the stairs with all the grace and dignity that befits the "daughter of a thousand jeddaks," while the two accompanying bodyguards are having their problems. The warrior on the right has one arm outthrust as if to balance himself, and he is looking down at his feet; the other guard has one hand on the wall for support, and he is peering around the corner to see if anyone is watching him.

tak: {LG-4/11} A Barsoomian unit of time equal to fifty tals, or 44.25 seconds of Earth time. ("Tak" will not be found in the canon but has been created to supplant what John Carter refers to as a "tal" in *Llana of Gathol*, Bk. 4, Chap. 11, when he says there are "four tals to a xat" whereas his earlier table, in *The Gods of Mars*, Chap. 16, shows 200 tals to a xat.)

tal: {GM/16; WM/3; LG-4/11} A Barsoomian unit of time, being 1/200 of a xat, or .885 of a second. When describing a Barsoomian clock — in *Llana of Gathol*, Bk. 4, Chap. 11 — Carter states there are four tals to a xat. This is an obvious error, possibly one of translation by Burroughs.

tan: Barsoomian word meaning "one hundred." *E.g.*, tanpi = 100 pi.

tanpi: {LG-2/11} An oval-shaped coin of gold, comparable to a U.S. dollar.

tee: Barsoomian word meaning "ten." *E.g.*, teepi = ten cents.

teeay: Barsoomian word for "eleven." Or: tee ("ten") + ay ("one").

teedwar: {FMM/1} A military rank between a dwar and an odwar. Thus, he would command a dar of one thousand men.

teepi: {LG-2/11} An oval-shaped coin of silver, comparable to the U.S. ten-cent piece.

Temple of Beauty, the: {CM/9} A great art gallery in Helium, wherein are displayed paintings, sculpture, and other examples of the creative arts.

Temple of Issus, the: {GM/8+} The palace of Issus, goddess of the First Born. It lies in the Valley Dor, on the shores of the Lost Sea of Korus.

Temple of Knowledge, the: {FMM/2} A library or archives in Helium where, among other things, are maintained replicas or pictures of the metal and harness of every known nation of Barsoom.

Temple of Reward, the: {GM/16; WM/16} A magnificent structure in Greater Helium, facing the Avenue of Ancestors. A hall of justice. "It is here that Martian justice is meted to benefactor and malefactor. Here the hero is decorated. Here the felon is condemned" *(GM/16)*. It is a vast, circular coliseum divided by the Aisle of Hope, which leads to the Throne of Righteousness and the Pedestal of Truth.

Temple of the Sun, the: {GM/20+; WM/1,3} A small pantheon or shrine in the heart of the Temple of Issus, in the Valley Dor. Topped by a slender, jewel-encrusted, golden spire, it has at its base—deep beneath the surface—687 chambers, one above the other. To each chamber a single corridor leads through solid rock from the pits of the Temple of Issus. The Temple of the Sun revolves with each revolution of Barsoom about the sun, and as a result the entrance to each chamber is opposite its particular corridor for only one day each year. These chambers or cells are used to incarcerate those who have incurred the wrath of Issus.

NOTE: Either Carter or Burroughs erred here. The proper number of chambers should be 668, the number of Barsoomian days in a year, and not 687, which is the number of Earth days equal to a Barsoomian year.

Tenth Cycle: {GM/4} A rank high among the order of Holy Therns.

than: {LG-3/6} Barsoomian word meaning "warrior." It applies equally to soldiers and sailors.

"Theoretical Mechanics": {SM/3} A technical book by an un-named Barsoomian author.

Third Jed, the: {SMM/10,11} A member of the Council of Seven Jeds, in Morbus. He eventually overthrew the other six, assumed sole command of Morbus, and took the name "Ay-mad."

Thoat: {CM/2, Appendix} A Jetan piece, representing a mounted warrior with two feathers. He can move two spaces, one straight and one diagonal, in any direction.

thorian: {GM/5} One of the highest ranks among the lesser therns. Possibly applied to a holder of the Ninth Cycle.

Throne of Righteousness, the: {GM/17; WM/16} A circular plat-form in the center of the great hall in the Temple of Reward in Greater Helium. About its perimeter are thirty-one chairs, upon which sit the judges, appointed by lot, to hear the accused or reward the hero. In its center is the Pedestal of Truth, whereon the individual stands while his case is being heard.

Thorian Tower, the: {CM/11} One of the turrets in the Towers of Jetan in the city of Manator. It was here that Tara of Helium was held captive.

tor: Barsoomian word for "four."

torches of Horz: {LG-1/6,8} A type of flashlight used by the Orovars of Horz but unknown to modern Barsoomians. "Cylindrical, they have a central core which glows brightly with a cold light when exposed to the air" *(LG-1/6)*. The more exposed, the brighter they shine. "The art of producing the central core was lost in far antiquity, and no scientist since has been able to analyze its composition" *(LG-1/6)*.

Tower of Diamonds, the: {SM/10-21} The central and tallest tower of the castle of the Tarids on Thuria. It contains the jeddak's quarters.

Tower of Thavas, the: {MMM/6,7; SMM/1} The original building erected by an ancestor of Ras Thavas some 23,000 years ago. It later became the center of a large complex, including Ras Thavas' extensive laboratories. It is situated on an island near the edge of the Great Toonolian Marshes, a few haads to the east of Toonol.

Towers of Jetan, the: {CM/11,13} A hollow square of buildings surrounding the Field of Jetan in the city of Manator, but in particular the several towers rising therefrom. The overseer holds the rank of dwar and is known as the Keeper of the Towers.

Tribute to Issus, the: {GM/11} The selection of a victim from those maidens who had served the cannibalistic Issus for a full year.

Tur: {MMM/10} The god of the Phundahlians, who believe his home is on the sun. One hundred thousand years ago, they say, he created Barsoom in the form of a disk, hurled it out into space, and then populated it with people, plants, and animals. His followers still insist the world is flat.

Turgan: {MMM/10} The sacred writings of Tur, god of the Phundahlians. To his followers, anything not found in the *Turgan* is not true.

Turquoise Tower, the: {SM/19,20} One of the towers of the castle of the Tarids, on Thuria. At least part of it serves as a prison.

umak: {FMM/F'word} A military unit of ten thousand men, commanded by an odwar.

utan: {GM/21; FMM/F'word} A military unit of one hundred men, under the command of a dwar.

Vanator: {CM/3,7} A Gatholian cruiser, pride of the fleet, and personal craft of Gahan, Jed of Gathol. Its loss in the great storm that swept across the planet is one of the unsolved mysteries of Barsoom.

Vosar: {MMM/7,8} One of the larger aircrafts in Ras Thavas' small fleet, commanded by Bal Zak of Toonol.

Warrior: {CM/2, Appendix} A Jetan piece, representing a foot soldier with two feathers. He can move two spaces straight or diagonally, in any direction.

xat: {GM/16, WM/3} A Barsoomian unit of time, equal to 2.95 minutes Earth time. There are fifty xats to a zode.

Xavarian: {GM/16} A ship of the fleet of Helium, under Kantos Kan, commander of the fleet.

Yano: {FMM/12} One of the oldest games of chance played by Barsoomians. It is composed of tiny, numbered spheres that are rolled across a board containing numbered holes, and is very popular with the troops.

zode: {GM/16; FMM/2} A Barsoomian unit of time, one tenth of a Barsoomian day, and containing fifty xats. It is equal to 2.462 Earth hours.

Chapter VIII — Quotations, Proverbs, and Expletives—From the Rich Heritage of Barsoom and the Pen of John Carter

It is hoped that the compiling of these quotations, maxims, and expletives—arranged in chronological order from the eleven-book series—will add due luster to the *oeuvre* of Edgar Rice Burroughs. No doubt the list is incomplete, and probably burdened with some trivia, but it does open the door on a fresh phase of Barsoomian lore. Here can be found beauty, humor, bitterness, anger—the gamut of emotions—as expressed by the people of Barsoom (soldier, scientist, savage, etc.) and by the Warlord of Mars, John Carter. May it prove both enjoyable and rewarding.

"...the Martians are a happy people; they have no lawyers." {PM/9}
Indicative of Burroughs' distaste for legal technicalities.

"A warrior may change his metal, but not his heart." {PM/13}
A saying common throughout Barsoom.

"...a creature who could not polish the teeth of her grandmother's sorak."{PM/14}
Equivalent to "not fit to polish my shoes."

"Give a Martian woman a chance and death must take a back seat." {PM/15}
John Carter, referring to the Tharkian women's skill at healing the wounded.

"...a man's way with women is in inverse ratio to his prowess among men." {PM/16}
Carter's opinion of himself as a suitor.

"...I had but jumped from purgatory into gehenna." {PM/18}

An expression, obviously Earthly, used by Carter.

"In the name of the ninth day..." {PM/20}
An expression of surprise or wonder, used by the old keeper of the Atmosphere Plant. (Some ERB scholars feel this should read "ninth ray." "Ninth day" has no significance, whereas the "ninth ray" is the vital one from which Barsoom's atmosphere is produced.)

"By the mother of the further moon..." {PM/21}
A mild form of Barsoomian profanity.

"That Tardos Mors may meet the greatest living warrior of Barsoom is a priceless honor, but that he may lay his hand on the shoulder of a friend and ally is a far greater boon." {PM/26}
The sincere acknowledgment of friendship from Tardos Mors to Tars Tarkas.

"I know that you are interested and that you believe, and I know that the world, too, is interested, though they will not believe for many years; yes, for many ages, since they cannot understand." {GM/F'word}
Carter's words to his nephew in 1898, when handing over the manuscript of his early adventures on Barsoom.

"This is the valley of love and peace and rest to which every Barsoomian since time immemorial has longed to pilgrimage at the end of a life of hate and strife and bloodshed." {GM/3}
Tars Tarkas' description of the Barsoomian paradise.

"We are between the wild thoat of certainty and the mad Zitidar of fact..."{GM/3}
Barsoomian equivalent to "between the devil and the deep blue sea."

"There is no hope, there is no hope, the dead return not, the dead return not, nor is there any resurrection. Hope not, for there is no hope." {GM/3}

Thern warning to those who reach the Valley Dor in the belief it is Heaven.

"Leave to a Thark his head and one hand and he may yet conquer." {GM/4}
An ancient Tharkian proverb, expressing the courage and tenacity of their tribe.

"The one on whom all responsibility rests is apt to endure the most." {GM/7}
An observation made by Carter following a brush with death.

"...the lower orders that stupidly float down an unknown river to an unknown end..." {GM/8}
The contempt shown by Phaidor, daughter of the Holy Hekkador, for the Barsoomians of the outside world.

"Blessed be the shell of thy first ancestor..." {GM/8}
A form of greeting among the First Born.

"I must have inherited from my father a wild lust for adventure, as well as a hollow where my bump of reverence should be." {GM/10}
Carthoris' defense of his inherited recklessness.

"My sword, my body, my life, my soul are yours to do with as you wish. Until death and after death I look to you alone for authority for my every act. Be you right or wrong, your word shall be my only truth. Whoso raises his hand against you must answer to my sword." {GM/16}

The oath of fealty sometimes paid to an outstanding and popular jeddak, but seldom, if ever, to a lesser mortal.

"...you know best the promptings of your own heart. That I shall need your sword I have little doubt, but accept from John Carter upon his sacred honor the assurance that he will never call upon you to

draw this sword other than in the cause of truth, justice, and right-eousness." {GM/16}
An appropriate reply to the above assertion, as expressed by John Carter.

"...that pitiful purgatory peopled by the poor unfortunates who dare not continue their abandoned pilgrimage to Dor..." {WM/4}
Carter's description of the Valley of Lost Souls.

"...the silent line of destruction and death..." {WM/6}
Carter's description of the green warriors in ambush outside the walls of Kaol.

"...I do not intend to be led, like a decrepit thoat to the slaughter..." {WM/7}
Carter's protest, when ordered to leave Kaol.

"...the 'forbidden land'..." {WM/8}
A Barsoomian term for that unknown area beyond the ice barrier that surrounds the north polar region.

"Man builds naught that man may not destroy." {TMM/2}
Observation made by a skilled artificer of Dusar.

"...blessed be your ancestors..." {TMM/13}
A Barsoomian form of salutation.

"Why attempt to explain the inexplicable?" {CM/Prel.}
A statement by Carter when asked to explain his agelessness.

"My sword is at your feet..." {CM/1; See also LG-1/10}
A Barsoomian expression meaning "I am at your service. You have my loyalty." It is a formality when merely spoken, but is a solemn oath when accompanied by the actual placing of the sword.

"We... speak... with tongues of steel rather than of flesh." {CM/1}
How a Gatholian warrior would "converse" with his enemies.

"I have the disposition of a thoat..." {CM/2}

"I am in a contrary mood." Thoats are noted for their short tempers.

"I still live!" {CM/2}

Spoken by Tara of Helium after she was swept away in the great storm. The remark, however, is attributed to her father, John Carter, who used it whenever facing what seemed to be a hopeless situation.

"...dons the leather of the dead..." {CM/3}

An expression used when one sets out on what is probably a suicidal mission.

"...mad queen of heaven!" {CM/4}

A description of Thuria, the fast-moving, nearer moon of Barsoom.

"...Thuria left the heavens to her lord and master, hurrying on to keep her tryst with the Sun in other skies." {CM/4}

Romantic fantasy of the "eternal triangle": Thuria, the wife and coquette; Cluros, the cold husband; and Sol, the brazen paramour.

"Came Thuria again and after a while the great Sun—a flaming lover, pursuing his heart's desire. And Cluros, the cold husband, continued his serene way, as placid as before his house had been violated by this hot Lothario." {CM/4}

Continuing the allegorical description of the heavenly bodies over Barsoom.

"Shadow of [my] first ancestor!" {CM/4}

An exclamation of dismay.

"...if one of them ever dropped his egotism and broke it it would take a week to fumigate Helium." {CM/6}

An expression attributed to Carter when speaking of a clique of self-styled intellectuals.

"...absolute perfection is as little to be desired as is its antithesis." {CM/6}

Thought expressed by Tara of Helium while a prisoner of the kaldanes in Bantoom.

"Let whoso would revert to nothingness impede me." {CM/8}

Spoken by Ghek as he prepared to fight his way out of the apartment of the assassinated Luud.

"Thy reward shall surpass thy greatest desires." {CM/8}
(and)

"...to serve thus a red woman of Barsoom is in itself sufficient reward."

Courtesies exchanged between Tara of Helium and her rescuer, despite the stress and danger.

"The Gods sent you." {CM/8}
Appreciation for a person arriving at the opportune time.

"By my first ancestor!" {CM/10}
A simple Barsoomian oath.

"We might even walk with God in the garden of His stars while man was still but a budding idea within His mind." {CM/12}
Spoken by Carter to ERB when commenting on a kaldane's ability to recall impressions and experiences of his forebears.

"...the head is useless when the heart usurps its functions..." {CM/14}
Love and reason are often incompatible, as Turan the panthan discovers.

"When a man chooses to hide his identity behind an assumed name, whatever friend pierces the deception were no friend if he divulged the other's secret." {CM/18}
Spoken by A-Sor, or Tasor, when he recognized Gahan of Gathol in the corridors of the palace in Manator.

"Your integrity has perceived and your lips voiced an unalterable truth." {CM/18}
Gahan's reply to A-Sor's observation above. These are fine examples of the courtliness of Barsoomian speech, regardless of circumstances or surroundings.

"You have no right to assume aught else than my lips testify." {CM/18}
Tara of Helium to Turan the panthan.

"The eyes are ofttimes more eloquent than the lips..." {CM/18}

Turan's reply to the above statement by Tara.

"To be abused, even, by the mistress of one's heart is better than to be ignored." {CM/18}

Turan's meager satisfaction upon hearing Tara express concern over his safety.

"...there be finer and nobler things than perfect mentality uninfluenced by the unreasoning tuitions of the heart." {CM/20}

An observation or admission by Ghek the kaldane.

"...the voiceless message in the air..." {CM/20}

O-Tar's way of saying that rumors are circulating.

"You and a few others of the chosen will believe in it — for the rest it matters not as yet. The time will come..." {MMM/A Letter}

Prophetic words by Ulysses Paxton, in his letter to Burroughs, dated June 8, 1925. Did he foresee the rise of ERB fandom some thirty to forty years later?

"Death, only, renders hope futile." {MMM/4}

Spoken by Ulysses Paxton (Vad Varo) to Valla Dia, who despaired of ever recovering her own body.

"I admire the will, but fear that the flesh is without sufficient strength." {MMM/8}

Spoken by Bal Zak when he was told that Vad Varo and his companions would go to any lengths to escape.

"War never brought peace — it but brings more and greater wars. War is Nature's natural state — it is folly to combat it." {MMM/9}

An observation by Mu Tel of Toonol when he was told by Ulyssess Paxton that World War I was fought for peace.

"There is no question about it, John Carter." {MMM/14}

The first words spoken by one American to another on the planet Barsoom. They were said, in English, by Ulysses Paxton on the deck of the flagship of the Phundahlian fleet.

"Her... [Sanoma Tora's] beauty... differs from that of Dejah Thoris as the chaste beauty of a polar landscape differs from the beauty of the tropics, as the beauty of a white palace in the moonlight differs from the beauty of its garden at midday." {FMM/1}

Tan Hadron's comparison of two of Helium's most beautiful women.

"...dark as the depths of Omean..." {FMM/4}
The equivalent to our "as dark as pitch."

"Our ancestors are with us to-night." {FMM/4}
An expression of luck or good fortune.

"May my ancestors forgive me!" {FMM/5}
An expression of self-reproach.

"The blind philosophy of absolute courage..." {FMM/6}
Nur An's impression of John Carter's motto, "I still live."

"...even yet there is a germ of hope within me that even utter hope-lessness cannot destroy." {FMM/8}
A desperate prayer by Sharu of Ghasta, to not give up.

"...until I am gathered to my ancestors your image shall remain en-shrined within my heart." {FMM/9}
Sham's farewell to Hadron of Hastor.

"...first thoughts are often inspirations, while sober afterthought may lead to failure, or so delay action as to nullify all its effect." {FMM/11}
A lengthy equivalent to our "He who hesitates is lost."

"Blood of our first ancestor!" {FMM/12}
A Barsoomian oath.

"...you shall find a home in the house of my father and a mother in my mother." {FMM/14}

Tan Hadron's platonic (he thought) offer of a home to the homeless Tavia.

"I was playing a game with Death, and I must give him no advantage." {SM/3}
John Carter, when seeking out the assassins of Zodanga.

"Nonchalance is a corollary of poise." {SM/7}
Carter's equivalent to "Keep cool."

"Cluros, the farther moon, rode high in the heavens, lighting dimly the streets of Zodanga like a dusty bulb in a huge loft..." {SM/8}
Carter's description of the faint moonlight.

"Eyes speak the truth more often than the lips." {SM/9}
Carter's thoughts when Rapas was lying to him.

"Your suspicions were well founded and your reasoning faultless." {SMM/6}
Carter, when identified by Ras Thavas.

"Some day I shall create the perfect man, and a new race of supermen will inherit Barsoom..." {SMM/7}
A boast by Ras Thavas.

"You haven't the brains of a sorak." {SMM/7}
A Barsoomian term of contempt.

"If there is an Almighty God he may resent this usurpation of his prerogatives." {SMM/7}
Carter, when speaking of Ras Thavas' attempt to create human life.

"The last of the great oceans... Its eventual passing will doubtless mark the passing of a world, and Mars will hurtle on through all eternity peopled by not even a memory of its past grandeur." {SMM/30}
Musings of Carter as he cruised over the lagoons and islets of the Great Toonolian Marshes.

"The fate of a friend transcends that of a planet." {SMM/30}
Carter's philosophy that the immediate problem often blocks out the more vital issue.

"It is the character that makes the man, not the clay which is its abode." {SMM/30}

Equivalent to our "Handsome is as handsome does."

"No matter how instinctively gregarious one may be there are times when one longs for solitude." {LG-1/1}
Carter, commenting on his need to be alone at times.

"The knowledge and the arts of the ancients are beyond the ken of modern man." {LG-1/5}
A statement by Pan Dan Chee — in the pits of Horz.

"I want to make more than enough to feed my wife's sorak." {LG-2/7}
Equivalent to our "I expect more than chicken feed."

"Moping seems to be the natural state of all lovers." {LG-3/1}
Carter, commenting on Pan Dan Chee's affection for Llana of Gathol.

"...he's as mean as an ulsio." {LG-3/5}
A Panarian warrior's description of Phor San.

"...that son of a calot..." {LG-3/5}
As a calot is the Barsoomian equivalent of a dog, the inference is obvious.

"If it has happened or is going to happen, the market place knows it." {LG-3/11}
An old Panarian saying.

"The lesser peoples of Barsoom are great braggarts..." {LG-4/2}

At Carter learned, the more backward or the less powerful the nation, the more they boasted.

"My deepest reverence for whichever one of your ancestors gave you a sense of humor." {LG-4/4}

Ptor Fak's appreciation of Carter's ability to make light of his troubles.

"We have the Princess." {LG-4/8}

A term borrowed from the game of Jetan. It is equivalent to our "It's in the bag."

"The city was quite as depressing in appearance as is Salt Lake City from the air on an overcast February day." {JCM(SMJ)/3}

Carter's description of Morgor City on Jupiter. However, I feel it is more likely ERB's interpretation, for when did *Carter* fly over Salt Lake City? (Burroughs flew over Salt Lake City in February 1927, as will be seen by his letter of June 30, 1930, to William L. Chenery of the P. F. Collier & Son Co. See *ERB-dom*, #70, dated May 1973, in this regard.)

"They might have... risen from sad graves to rattle their bones in mock life in a cemetery city of the dead." {JCM(SMJ)/3}

Carter's description of the pedestrians of Morgor City.

"You could not possibly conceive any terms of opprobrium in which to describe them more virulent than those which I have long used and considered inadequate." {JCM(SMJ)/4}

Words alone could not express Zan Dar's contempt for the Morgors.

"But wars are not won by defensive methods." {JCM(SMJ)/4}

Zan Dar, admitting the inability of his people to defeat the raiding Morgors.

"The Morgors, like death, were without art." {JCM(SMJ)/4}

Carter, when mentioning the lack of decorations and appointments in the Morgor palace.

"It was as though Death had looked upon me and singled me out as his own." {JCM(SMJ)/4}
How Carter felt when Bandolian, the Morgor chief, first looked at him.

"While you live, hope will live," {JCM(SMJ)/5}
Dejah Thoris, when she found that Carter still lived.

"Hope, almost extinct, leaped to life again." {JCM(SMJ)/9}
 Carter, when he saw an opportunity to seize a Morgor ship.

Chapter IX — Barsoomian Science and Invention

It is interesting to look at the scientific achievements credited to the Barsoomians by Edgar Rice Burroughs, who presented them to us in 1912 (although they were originally recorded by John Carter, when preparing his first manuscript, in his cottage on the banks of the Hudson River in the decade 1876-1886). I have set them out, roughly, in the order of appearance in the series.

Only moments after Carter found himself on Barsoom, he came face to face with a band of green warriors armed with rifles, the long barrels of which were made of an alloy of aluminium and steel. These weapons, which discharge small-caliber, explosive radium projectiles, have an amazing range of three hundred miles. {PM/3}

(NOTE: Burroughs uses the word "radium" only because it was the nearest Earth substance to that described by Carter.)

These same green men had, besides candles and torches, oil lamps that gave off a far-reaching, white light. {PM/5}

The transplanted Virginian was told by the Heliumatic princess, Dejah Thoris, that Barsoomians had developed telescopic cameras which could take pictures of Earth objects as small as a blade of grass. {PM/11}

He also learned of wonderful healing and remedial powders and ointments that could heal any wound, however severe. {PM/15}

Following his escape from the Tharks, and the Warhoons, Carter sought shelter in a great structure which he learned produced the life-sustaining air so vital to the planet. He discovered that the Barsoomian spectrum contained nine primary colors, two more than those known to Earthmen, and that these possessed strange properties. The eighth ray, he learned, was known as the ray of propulsion. It was a force of repulsion of gravity, which, when isolated and stored, could lift almost any weight from the surface of the planet. The ninth ray—when isolated, treated, and released—combines with the ether of space to form the atmosphere of Barsoom. {PM/20,21}

In Zodanga, Kantos Kan treated Carter to his first restaurant meal—in an automat. Here the meal was "served entirely by mechanical apparatus. No hand touched the food from the time it entered the building in its raw state until it emerged hot and delicious upon the tables before the guests, in response to the touching of tiny buttons to indicate their desires." {PM/21}

It was in Zodanga that Carter became familiar with a form of Barsoomian aircraft. Buoyed by the eighth Barsoomian ray, the light one-man ship is propeller-driven by a compact, noiseless, radium engine at speeds exceeding two hundred miles per hour. It is equipped with a compass that, when set, points to the place of intended arrival. Naval vessels, he discovered, range in size from the one-man flier to troop ships and dreadnoughts armed with mighty guns and a crew of thousands. {PM/21}

John Carter returned to Earth — of his own choice this time — in May or June of 1898, and wrote another series of papers describing life in general and his adventures in particular on the planet Barsoom. These he handed to his nephew, Edgar Rice Burroughs, who in turn passed a portion on to his many readers, who accepted it as entertaining fiction. We learn of more inventions and developments on this other world, instant photocopying being but one of the marvels described. {GM/F'word}

While trailing Matai Shang and Thurid through the corridors under the Otz Mountains, Carter was temporarily delayed by a locked door. After studying it, he discovered that the mechanism was controlled by a series of light rays of varying intensity for certain lengths of time. {WM/3}

Deep within the arctic wastes, he found, the yellow-skinned Okarians had defied the frigid conditions with great glass-domed cities heated by the sun's rays, which were captured, stored in huge reservoirs, and released as needed. {WM/9} The Okarians also had a machine which measured, weighed, and photographed a person — all at the same time. Copies of the result were reproduced instantly in offices in different, widely separated cities. {WM/10}

Carthoris, with the restless, challenging brain inherited from his father, improved on the aircraft destination compass by adding a device that steered the craft on the intended course and stopped it when it reached its destination, thus making the whole trip automatic. {TMM/1}

At the same time, others were at work improving aircraft motors, and a speed of over three hundred miles per hour — or two thousand haads per zode — had been attained. It was only a matter of time before a properly constructed flier would be exceeding one thousand miles per hour (seven thousand haads per zode). {FMM/2}

The people of Helium commuted between the Twin Cities by means of pneumatic tubes. A person would enter an eight-foot-long bullet-shaped car, indicate his destination on a dial, lie down, and almost immediately the carrier would move off, enter a tube, and within seconds emerge onto another platform some seventy-five miles from the point of embarkation. {TMM/2}

(From here on, the information I have set out was received first-hand, orally, from John Carter, or direct from Barsoom via the Gridley Wave.)

The most common interior-lighting system for civilized Barsoomi-ans is by means of heavy, glass, hemispherical bowls set in wall or ceiling and containing a substance or compound of a radium-like na-ture. This form of lighting had been perfected so long ago that its ori-gin was lost in antiquity. The light itself was capable of lasting for centuries without any noticeable loss of intensity. {CM/4}

The cities of Barsoom possess unique street lights. The controlled "light waves leave the lamp, pass along a prescribed circuit and re-turn to the lamp. There is no waste nor... are there any dense shad-ows... for the waves, in passing around objects to return to the lamp, illuminate all sides of them." {MMM/8}

Ras Thavas, the great Toonolian scientist and surgeon, wore multi-lensed spectacles and a hearing aid of his own design; and was skilled at transplanting human organs, both internal and external, from one person to another. He has, on many occasions, transferred a human brain from one cranium to another. {MMM/1-4}

His assistant, Vad Varo—perhaps better known to us as Ulysses Paxton of the U.S.A.—was performing heart transplants in Ras Tha-vas' laboratory as early as, if not before, the year 1920 Earth time. {MMM/4}

It was Ras Thavas who told Vad Varo that Barsoomian scientists had confirmed that intelligent life exists on Mercury and Venus, and that studies had been made of thought waves from the inhabitants of those worlds. The nature of the instruments used in these endeavors was not disclosed. {MMM/2}

When in Toonol, Paxton encountered the equilibrimotor: a broad belt inflated with a sufficient amount of the eighth Barsoomian ray to equalize the pull of gravity. A small motor is attached to the rear of the belt, and controls to the front. From each side extend strong, light wings equipped with hand levers to aid in flight. {MMM/8}

It was in 1929, Earth time, that successful radio communication was made between Barsoom and Earth. Jason Gridley's (see also *Tanar of Pallucidar*) unique radio wave had been picked up by scientists at Helium, and in time they were able to duplicate it and reply. It was thus that we learned of the great new advances in aeronautics on Barsoom, and were told of the inventions of that frustrated and slightly demented Jaharian scientist, Phor Tak. {FMM/F'word}

It was Phor Tak who made the rifle that projected disintegrating rays capable of destroying whatever metal to which it has been attuned. He followed this with a paint which dissipated the ray, thus creating a protective coat for defensive purposes. Quarreling with his jeddak, Phor Tak fled from Jahar and set up his own workshop, where he invented an airborne missile, the Flying Death, which would seek out enemy craft, overtake, and destroy them. As a protective measure, he developed a paint which, when applied to an object, made it invisible by causing light rays to bend around it. {FMM/5,10}

The missile, the rifle, and its ammunition were destroyed by Tan Hadron of Hastor; and, with the death of Phor Tak, there seems little likelihood of their redevelopment. {FMM/17}

Two Zodangan scientists, Fal Sivas and Gar Nal, came out with spaceships at virtually this same time, but that of Fal Sivas was by far the superior. It contained a mechanical brain that responded to the thought waves of the pilot and could be controlled either from within or from outside the ship. {SM/5}

Ras Thavas, the Master Mind of Mars, had not been idle. Driven from his home near Toonol, he set up his laboratory on an island in the great marsh and proceeded to experiment with the development of synthetic human life. He both succeeded and failed. His creations were less than perfect, and the more advanced rebelled against their creator, causing him to flee. The vats of half-formed "hormads" went unattended and commenced to grow without restriction or order. Ras Thavas was forced to call upon the navy of Helium to destroy his

work with a deluge of firebombs, and he abandoned all further ex-
perimentation. {SMM/7+}

The Morgors of Sasoom, or Jupiter, have developed spaceships capable of traveling at speeds exceeding twenty-three miles a second.
They accomplished this through use of "the ray of propulsion, in
combination with the highly concentrated gravitational forces of all
celestial bodies within the range of whose attraction the ship passes,
and a concentration of Ray L (cosmic rays) which are collected from
space and discharged at high velocities from propulsion tubes at the
ship's stern." {JCM(SMJ)/3}

Sasoom's beaches provide a submicroscopic, magnetic sand composed of prismatic crystals which, when sprayed over a metallic object, cause light rays to bend around it—thus making it invisible. The
Morgors use this substance, Carter discovered, to conceal their aircraft; whereas the more peace-loving inhabitants of the planet use it to
camouflage their homes. {JCM(SMJ)/2}

Chapter X – Through Space to Barsoom!

When considering the likelihood of reaching Mars, we are inclined to wonder if the space travelers will first see the polar ice caps, then the rolling ochre sea bottoms, as well as the vast stretch of green swamp that forms the Great Toonolian Marshes. As they near the planet, will the cities of Helium, Ptarth, and Gathol come into view? The answer is "No" — for Mars is not Barsoom. There is a connection, a certain something in common; yet they are not one and the same globe. One cannot get to Barsoom by sailing outward from Earth in a mundane spacecraft. John Carter passed into another dimension to reach his beloved Barsoom, as did Ulysses Paxton; although neither seemed to realize this, each believing he was on that red planet he had gazed at so often from Earth.

Had Carson Napier's takeoff from Guadalupe (in Burroughs' *Pirates of Venus*) been better calculated, he might have reached Mars as planned. But it would not have been Barsoom.

Jason Gridley's discovery of a new form of radio wave (in ERB's *Tanar of Pellucidar*) enabled him to penetrate into this other dimension — without his realizing it — and thus open communication, not with Mars, but with the people of Barsoom. Although we were entertained with the tales of adventure on the Red Planet, no one really believed them and the Gridley Wave was laughed off as pure fiction.

Some forty years later, Barsoomian scientists accidentally discovered a wave that was picked up here on Earth on a normal band, and radio communication between Earth and Barsoom became a reality (ERB's *The Moon Maid*).

The spaceship that left Barsoom for Earth in 2015, Earth time *(The Moon Maid)*, was doomed before it started, for it had no way of moving from its dimension to ours. *The Barsoom*, which left Earth on Christmas Day, 2025 (in the same book), stood no better chance; and its commander, Julian 5th, might have gone to his death on that barren, empty world we know as Mars, had he not been diverted to our own moon instead.

Sasoom is not Jupiter, but rather its counterpart in that other, "Barsoomian" dimension. Thus the Morgor spaceship used to kidnap John Carter could travel between Sasoom and Barsoom, but could not have gone on to Earth; although it possibly could have reached Jasoom, Earth's counterpart, of which we — up to now — know nothing.

This matter of dimensions also explains why Carter could not transport himself from Zodanga to Thuria to rescue Dejah Thoris (*Swords of Mars*) in the same manner he traveled between Barsoom and the United States. Similarly, he could not return from Sasoom to Helium (*John Carter of Mars/Skeleton Men of Jupiter*). These places were in the same dimension, and his strange power worked only when moving from one dimension to another.

Carter himself seemed quite unaware of this, and his statement in the Foreword to *The Gods of Mars* — "I have learned the secret, nephew, and I may traverse the trackless void at my will, coming and going between the countless planets as I list" — was merely an opinion, one he had never attempted to verify.

Chapter XI – "Edgar Rice Burroughs": A Brief Biographical Sketch

of the man who through his unique relationship with John Carter of Virginia, Warlord of Barsoom, was able to give us those thrilling accounts of life on another planet.

There were two Edgar Rice Burroughses. The one with whom we are better acquainted has been widely recognized and acclaimed. Briefly: we know he was born in Chicago in 1875 and died at Encino, California, in 1950, leaving a daughter and two sons. However, this is not his story.

The second Edgar Rice Burroughs was another man, indeed. His life history, as set out below, was gleaned mainly from the Prologues, Introductions, Preludes, and Forewords of the Mars and other books produced by the first-mentioned individual, and from an occasional dip into the books themselves.

To establish the year of Burroughs' birth the reader must turn to the Foreword in the initial Mars book *(A Princess of Mars)*, where he will find the following: "My first recollection of Captain Carter is of the few months he spent at my father's home in Virginia, just prior to the opening of the civil war. I was then a child of but five years."

A few months prior to the opening of the Civil War would be the latter part of 1860, which means that the writer of the above quotation was born in 1855.

Little is known of his early life except that his parents operated a plantation near Richmond, Virginia, where they were known to have possessed a fine stable of horses and the usual stock of slaves. Doubtless, most of this was lost during the campaigning.

By the late 1870's, Burroughs, in partnership with his father, had succeeded in building up a string of general stores throughout the state. In 1886, he inherited, not only a considerable fortune from his great-uncle—the aforementioned Captain Carter—but also a manuscript dealing with that great Virginian's strange adventures on the planet Mars, or Barsoom, as it is know to its inhabitants.

Carter's will specified that this manuscript was not to be unsealed until 1897 and its contents not divulged to the rest of the world until 1907. However, Burroughs opened the documents at once *(The Gods of Mars)*, read it, and released it in book form shortly thereafter. No reason is given for this rather surprising breach of trust, nor did Carter show any resentment when they next met.

During this time, and through to the end of the century, Burroughs was still residing at the old homestead, which lay some two hours by rail from the state capital. It was at Richmond in the year 1898 that he and John Carter were reunited in what turned out to be the first of many visits. It was here that he was given the story of how Carter, upon his return to Barsoom, fought the length of a world to rescue his mate, Dejah Thoris, and ultimately become Warlord of Mars.

The next few years remain somewhat of a mystery. Burroughs *(The Outlaw of Torn)* is now married, and we know he visited Europe with his wife, around 1910, and that he carried out certain research at an old monastery to obtain material for a historical novel set in England during the reign of Henry III.

At the same time he made the acquaintance of an official at the British Colonial Office in London *(Tarzan of the Apes)*, and from him secured material and evidence covering the circumstances leading to the death of John Clayton, Lord Greystoke, and to the birth of his son, the future Tarzan of the Apes, in a cabin on the west coast of Africa.

We are aware that Burroughs became a close friend of Tarzan, Lord Greystoke *(The Eternal Lover)*, and that he was a guest at the Greystoke estate in British East Africa in 1913, during the visit there of Barney Custer and his sister, Victoria, of Beatrice, Nebraska.

From here he went on to North Africa to hunt lions, and doubtless he stopped off at a small west coast port to visit another friend, Herr Skopf, proprietor of the local hotel *(The Son of Tarzan)*.

At some period in this second decade, Burroughs moved to California, where he bought a ranch which he called "Tarzana," obviously in honor of his friend, Lord Greystoke.

Also, he received two visits from John Carter, Warlord of Mars (*Thuvia, Maid of Mars*). The first would be when he was told of the romance between Carthoris, son of the Warlord, and Thuvia of Ptarth. The second was several years later when Carter narrated the adventures of his daughter, Tara (*The Chessmen of Mars*). It is quite likely that this latter meeting was their first at "Tarzana."

In June 1916, Burroughs was back in North Africa (*Pellucidar*). This trip became imperative when he received a letter from one Cogden Nestor, who had found a telegraph instrument buried in the sands of the Sahara. Here, along with an English telegrapher, Frank Downes, they talked for some two months with David Innes in far-off Pellucidar.

All this activity must have been quite a strain on Mr. Burroughs, for in the summer of 1917 we find him up in Greenland (*The Land That Time Forgot*), vacationing on the advice of his doctor. While there, he plucked a thermos bottle from the ocean and in it found a message from one Bowen Tyler, who was marooned on the hitherto unknown island of Caspak, somewhere in the extreme southern Pacific. He thereupon made a quick trip back to civilization and to the Tyler home at Santa Monica, California. From here he sailed on the yacht *Toreador*, with Tom Billings, in search of Caspak and in an effort to rescue Tyler and his companions. Although he does not say so, it is quite likely that Burroughs actually entered Caspak with the men from the yacht and made the trip up the west coast to the land of the Galu.

By 1918, Burroughs had struck up a firm and lasting friendship with his neighbor, a young college graduate and radio enthusiast, Jason Gridley (*Tanar of Pellucidar*). It was through Gridley's inventive genius that they were able to contact Abner Perry in Pellucidar, and receive accounts of the happenings in this inner world.

Some time after the conclusion of hostilities in Africa, Burroughs paid a visit to Lord and Lady Greystoke (*Tarzan the Terrible*, Glossary) and learned of their wartime and Pal-ul-don adventures. It is not known if this visit took place in England or at Tarzan's African estate.

In 1925, Burroughs was treated with another visit from John Carter *(The Master Mind of Mars)*, who brought him a letter from the former Ulysses Paxton, now Vad Varo of Barsoom. In 1927 or 1928, he was in direct communication with Paxton by means of Gridley's radio *(A Fighting Man of Mars)*, which he was operating while Jason was on an expedition to Pellucidar.

It was in the year 1930 that Burroughs and his secretary, Ralph Rothmund, made the acquaintance of Carson Napier, a restless, wealthy adventurer *(Pirates of Venus)*. Burroughs eventually became Napier's only contact—through a form of mental telepathy—when the young man took off for Mars in a rocket ship and landed, instead, on Venus.

In order to escape boring social engagements and business pressures, Burroughs had acquired a cabin near the headwaters of the Little Colorado River in the White Mountains of Arizona *(Swords of Mars)*. He would often go there alone to rest and fish and just enjoy the quiet of the wilderness. Also it was his headquarters for solitary expeditions among the deserted canyons and crumbling cliffs where lay buried cities of a long-dead race. The great Apache chief, Geronimo, had roamed these mountains, as, too, had John Carter over fifty years before. Once, in the summer of 1934, Burroughs was joined at the cabin by Carter, from whom he heard further tales of adventure and romance on the Red Planet.

It was sometime in the mid-Thirties that Burroughs met Pat Morgan and learned the story of Jimber-Jaw ("The Resurrection of Jimber-Jaw"), a fifty-thousand-year-old cave man, known to most residents of the Arizona valley as Jim Stone.

In or about 1938, Burroughs was again in touch with Barsoom through the medium of the Gridley Wave *(Synthetic Men of Mars)*. By this means he learned of the serious injury to Dejah Thoris, and of Carter's desperate but successful efforts to secure the services of the master surgeon, Ras Thavas.

In 1940, Burroughs—now eighty-five years of age—was vacationing in Hawaii, on the island of Oahu, when he received his last recorded visit from John Carter *(Llana of Gathol)*; and this was their first since meeting at the cabin in the White Mountains of Arizona some six years earlier. Carter, he learned, was now a grandfather.

It was also at this time and place that phantom fingers on the Burroughs typewriter wrote of Poloda ("Beyond the Farthest Star"), a planet one-half million light-years from Earth, and of the adventures of a transplanted Earthman known only as Tangor.

We are not aware of how Burroughs came into possession of the facts concerning Carter's adventures on Sasoom (Jupiter); however, it is believed that the story was relayed via the Gridley Wave. But, through some unexplained accident, contact was broken before all the information had been received, and was never re-established.

Our next step is a long one, for we hear nothing more of this amazing man Burroughs until 1967 *(The Moon Maid)*. It was at the end of that great conflict which had been raging off and on since 1914. (As readers of *The Moon Maid* know, World War I did not end until about this date fifty years later.) While the masses were celebrating the peace, governments were going about their duties, trying to bring their affairs back to normal; and we find Burroughs on an air liner en route to Paris in 1967 on undisclosed business, at the remarkable age of one hundred and twelve.

Later, we learn he has been head of the United States Bureau of Communications for quite a number of years *(The Moon Men*, magazine version). In 1968, he took extended leave and went to Herschel Island in the Canadian Arctic, to hunt polar bears. A year later— March 1969, to be exact—when caught on an ice floe with a wounded bear, he was rescued by a cruiser of the newly formed International Peace Fleet. This very cruiser had been seeking him upon instructions of the President of the United States; for it seems the Secretary of Commerce had died suddenly, and Edgar Rice Burroughs—age one hundred fourteen!—had been offered the post, an offer which he accepted at once.

This is the final bit of information we have been able to uncover on this amazing man. We can only assume that he went on to serve his country in his own very capable manner. Where he is at the present time we do not know, nor do we know if he is still in touch with his old friends of this and other worlds.

Longevity! Without a doubt, it was in "ERB's" blood. John Carter mentioned this on the occasion of his visit to tell the story of Tara of Helium and Gahan of Gathol *(The Chessmen of Mars)*. He said. "You, yourself, have aged, though not as much as most men in a corresponding number of years, which may be accounted for by the fact that the same blood runs in our veins..." *(CM/Prel.)*. Much later, at Oahu, Carter made another statement *(Llana of Gathol)*. "After you are dead," he declared, "and it will not be long now, I shall have no Earthly ties..." *(LG/F'word)*. Happily for everyone, he proved to be a poor prophet in this particular instance.

John Carter himself was well over a hundred, yet he possessed the body of a man of thirty. Tarzan of the Apes reached maturity and then ceased to age, and the same applies to David Innes; whereas Carson Napier lives on, due to Venusian medical knowledge. Should it seem so strange that "Edgar Rice Burroughs," Master Story-Teller, Master of Adventure, and Master of Other Worlds is also Master of Time?

Acknowledgments and Sources

Clearly I became indebted to many people, in many ways, when compiling this book. Foremost, of course, is Edgar Rice Burroughs himself, for giving us the Mars sagas in the first place. I have taken the liberty of frequently using his own words when drawing up the definitions and descriptions, and I have not always used quotation marks when so doing.

It was a routine advertisement in the June 1957 *Science Fiction Adventures* that led me to the indefatigable Vernell Coriell and the Burroughs Bibliophiles organization. I owe much to Vernell for this initiation.

Camille Cazedessus, Jr., the energetic editor of *ERB-dom*, was responsible for my becoming a critic-writer-reviewer in the Burroughs field. This led to my meeting other editors, such as Pete Ogden of *Erbania*, Paul Allen of *Barsoomian*, and Phil Currie of *Erbivore*. Without these devotees and their magazines, this book could not have been written.

Others who must share the credit for the book are artists Neal MacDonald and Richard Robertson; also Henry Hardy Heins, John Harwood, Allan Howard; and, in particular, the late Frank Brueckel and his wife, Catherine, who aided me more than they may think.

A special thanks to Robert Hodes and Edgar Rice Burroughs, Inc., for recommending me to Betty Ballantine, and to Betty for giving me this opportunity.

Some of the material from which I drew valuable data and ideas was furnished by the following writers:

Allen, Paul C. "Ras Thavas," *Barsoomian,* #9 (July 1965).

Brueckel, Frank J. "A Map of Barsoom," *Burroughs Bulletin,* #14 (1963).

.... "Remarks on the Supernatural," *Barsoomian,* #13 (Jan. 1968).

.... "Barsoom, the Arctic Regions," *Erbivore,* #4 (Sept. 1968).

.... "Barsoom, the Antarctic Regions," *Erbivore,* #5 (March 1972).

Harwood, John (Jonhar Wud). "The Rise of John Carter," *Barsoomian,* #9 (July 1965).

.... A letter, *Erbivore,* Supp. Sept. 1970.

Howard, Allan. "The Bowman of Lothar," *Erbania,* #22 (Jan. 1968).

Huckenpahler, J. G. "A Glossary of Names and Terms Used in the Martian Stories," *ERB-dom,* #s 30 (Jan. 1970) through 41 (Dec. 1970).

Kwiecien, Fred. "Longevity & E.R.B.," *Barsoomian,* #10 (Jan. 1966).

.... "Supernaturally... E.R.B.," *Barsoomian,* #12 (Mar. 1967).

Resnick, Michael. "The History of Life on Barsoom," *ERB-dom,* #6 (April 1963).

.... "5 Barsoomian Maps," *ERB-dom,* #7 (July 1963).

.... "History of Life on Barsoom," *ERB-dom,* #44 (Mar. 1971).

Van Arnam, David, et al. *The Reader's Guide to Barsoom and Amtor.* New York: Richard Lupoff, 210 East 73rd Street; 1963.

The reader may also wish to refer to certain pertinent articles of my own which have appeared in the Hugo-winning (1966) fanzine *ERB-dom* over the past decade:

ERB-dom, #11 (Aug. 1964). "The Legendary Edgar Rice Burroughs."

#24 (Aug. 1968). "John Carter... Past and Present."

#26 (June 1969). "More on John Carter... Virginian."

#27 (Aug. 1969), "A Royal Map of Barsoom."

#65 (Dec. 1972). "Green Men of Barsoom."

From the Author

I was born on February 19, 1913, in Yarmouth, Nova Scotia, where the local library had most of the Burroughs novels. An avid reader, I soon became quite familiar with ERB's various creations.

After struggling through the early Thirties, I applied for the Royal Canadian Mounted Police and was accepted into that force in 1937. Thirty-four years later I retired, but during that time I maintained my interest in the Burroughs books.

Following my marriage in 1944, I began rebuilding my ERB library, and now I have two hundred hardcover editions, over a hundred paperbacks, and a few magazine versions. Add the fanzines, maps, and other miscellaneous items and you have a room full of Borroughsiana.

In 1958, I answered an ad about the "Burroughs Bibliophiles" and have been an active member of that group ever since. I soon learned of *ERB-dom, Erbania, Amra,* and other fanzines and have thoroughly relished reading them and writing for them.

Now retired, in Ridgetown, Ontario, I garden, golf, bowl, and generally enjoy my hundred-year-old house and the small-town life of rural southern Canada.

JFR
April 5, 1976

ReAnimus Press

Breathing Life into Great Books

If you enjoyed this book we hope you'll tell others or write a review! We also invite you to subscribe to our newsletter to learn about our new releases and join our affiliate program (where you earn 12% of sales you recommend) at www.ReAnimus.com.

Here are more ebooks you'll enjoy from ReAnimus Press, available from ReAnimus Press's web site, Amazon.com, bn.com, etc.:

Space Travel — A Guide for Writers,
by Ben Bova

The Star Conquerors, by Ben Bova
(Standard Edition and
Special Collector's Edition)

The Exiles Trilogy, by Ben Bova

Test of Fire, by Ben Bova

The Kinsman Saga, by Ben Bova

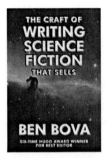

The Craft of Writing Science Fiction that Sells,
by Ben Bova

Staying Alive - A Writer's Guide,
by Norman Spinrad

Experiment Perilous: The 'Bug Jack Barron' Papers, an essay for writers by Norman Spinrad

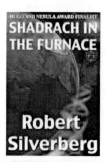

Shadrach in the Furnace, by Robert Silverberg

The Transcendent Man, by Jerry Sohl

Night Slaves, by Jerry Sohl

Bloom, by Wil McCarthy

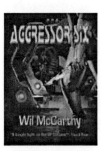

Aggressor Six, by Wil McCarthy

Murder in the Solid State,
by Wil McCarthy

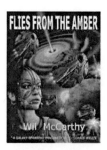

Flies from the Amber, by Wil McCarthy

Side Effects, by Harvey Jacobs

American Goliath, by Harvey Jacobs

"An inspired novel" – *TIME Magazine*
"A masterpiece...arguably this year's best novel" – *Kirkus Reviews*

CPSIA information can be obtained at www.ICGtesting.com
Printed in the USA
LVOW11s1951101014

408234LV00002BA/426/P